Tomorrow's Seduction:
KISS OF DEATH

a novel By
Warsan and Xperience J

ISBN-13 : 978-0615922881

ISBN-10 : 0615922880

Book Cover Design : Hot Book Covers
Photographed by : Andrew Gray
Model : Natasha "Breezy" Malone
Book Interior Design : Vedicdesign

Published
by
Two Pens and a Grind Publications
info@twopensandagrind.com

Printed in the United States of America

Tomorrow's Seduction:
KISS OF DEATH

XPERIENCE J'S
ACKNOWLEDGMENTS

To the Most High; your love is so unconditional! I am so undeserving and yet you see fit to bless me everyday. That's how I know this is what I was meant to do; no, that's how I know that this is who I was meant to be. Without you I am nothing, but with you, I can do anything! Thanks for the daily reminder that I am indeed a King's Kid!

To my mother: Words cannot express how grateful I am to call you my mother. I only pray that I can be half the woman/mother that you are one day. This is all for you! I grind hard everyday because I want to make sure that one day soon, you won't have a worry in the world because that's exactly what you've done for me! Even if it takes me a lifetime, I'm going to make sure that you're well taken care of! I love you!

To Taneckia, Markevia, and Taloni: You three have been the greatest friends I could ever ask for. More than friends, I consider you guys my sisters because I know there's nothing you wouldn't do for me and I feel the exact same way. Thanks for every call, prayer, and all of the well wishes and support throughout the years. There's a common stereotype amongst black women that says that we have a tendency to belittle and put each other down but you three are definitely exceptions to that rule because I've been nothing but uplifted and loved by all of you and I truly appreciate you!

To Family and Friends: With my first book I know I listed you guys individually but I'm sure that all of you know how much I care about you. Thanks for the continued support and I'm simply overwhelmed by just how much potential you see in me. All of you have your own grinds/hustles and are working just as hard (if not harder) than I am to make it out here and let me just tell you that you encourage me daily to step my game up so thank you!

To Tierra King aka Warsan: We have been friends since forever but I never thought in a million years that we would end up writing a book together! It all started from one silly conversation; reminiscing about the past and now, we're here at this moment! I'm so happy to be sharing this experience with you! Thanks for putting up with all my antics and all of the late night phone calls and hard work we've put into EVERY venture we've pursued. The name "Two Pens and a Grind" is an understatement because we've put blood, sweat, and tears into birthing this movement and I can't wait for the outcome!

To the cast/crew/affiliates of Two Pens and a Grind: I so appreciate your hard work and helping us build this movement from the ground up. Without you, this definitely wouldn't have been possible. You guys grind so hard for us without asking much of anything. You personify what true teamwork and networking is all about. I'm glad to have you guys on my team…and even more grateful that you guys have become my friends! We did it!

And last but definitely NOT least:

To my people on the grind, this one is for you! Don't stop grinding! If it's yours, go get it! What God has for you, is for you and NO ONE can ever take that away!

Be Blessed Yall,

Xperience J

WARSAN'S
ACKNOWLEDGMENTS

I give all my thanks to my father "Almighty God" and to my dear children; Tanauz, Tamir, Wali and the late Warsan, thank you for bringing out the strength inside of me I never knew I had. Rest in peace Warsan! With God you're in good hands now. To my immediate family: Catherine King, Kellie King-Scott, Mike Scott, Keisha Williams and Keia Reddick I love you all.

P.S. Shout out to Jasmine Elliot, Deanna Owens and my girl Crystal Judkins aka Xperience J for staying true friends and always keeping it real even when I didn't want to hear it. You three were there through all of my darkest hours and I can't thank you enough.

Also I would like to give a special thanks to everyone who helped bring Two Pens and a Grind together from scratch. Yes you! All the actors, film crew, editors and designers, I LOVE YOU and thanks for your part in bringing my vision to reality.

And to my fans… Always remember "Man says no but God says yes!"

Warsan

PROLOGUE

"You crazy bitch! Untie me before —"

The smell of nicotine filled the air. The room was dark and only her silhouette could be identified. A crazy sex session had gone terribly wrong and Craig knew that he was going to die.

He would become the latest victim of the Kiss of Death Serial Killer in a matter of moments. How had this happened? Like many others, Craig had fallen prey to her deception. She was beautiful, witty, and sex-crazed; a cocktail for the perfect woman. She could easily entice any guy with whom she came in contact, and she usually did.

There was just one thing that her admirers hadn't bet on: she was a stone cold killer with an appetite for blood and destruction.

She had Craig butt naked and tied up to the bed post in his room. The fact that she had so much power made her pussy wet, but her ultimate release wouldn't come until he was finally dead.

"Before what, nigga? All you muthafuckas are worthless." She laughed. *"Only good for one thing and to be honest, **that** wasn't even that good."*

"Fuck you, bitch!"

"You know, I think I'mma enjoy killing you the most, Craig." She giggled.

She flicked her cigarette butt in his direction and walked over to his chair. Craig's anger quickly turned to fear when she unveiled her 12" Dexter Russell butcher knife. She closed her eyes and seductively slid her *tongue down the middle of the knife.*

"Mmm, so fucking sexy ain't it?" she taunted.

Craig's eyes grew wide, but he didn't say a word. He closed his eyes and said a silent prayer, hoping that heaven was his next destination. She leaned in closer to him and smiled.

"Say an extra one for me," she gently whispered in his left ear before she repeatedly jabbed her knife deep inside his chest.

She finished the job with a single kiss to his forehead, leaving a trace of her Tom Ford Scarlet Rouge lipstick on his dying flesh.

She left Craig's apartment feeling liberated. Killing had become her latest and greatest pastime. Her two unspeakable sins were sex and murder, and without the two of them, she was nothing.

CHAPTER

~ 1 ~

Tomorrow raced her black 750 through the live streets of D.C. It was a dark and wet night, but she didn't care. She was on a mission. Her car reeked of cheap bourbon and thick hash, and the go-go band Backyard was bursting through her car's speakers. As she passed by nightclub after nightclub, people couldn't help but wonder who was flossing behind that Beamer with the five percent tinted windows.

She finally made it to Morse Street in Northeast and parked directly across from her destination. She stepped out of the car sporting her black and red mini fishnet dress, wearing only a g-string underneath. She knew she was dressed to kill, completing her outfit with the latest red-bottoms.

Before crossing the street, Tomorrow decided to finish off her fifth of Hennessy and smoke the rest of her blunt. She leaned against her driver's side door, taking her last few tokes and sipped her drink quickly.

She noticed her friend Legacy walking out of the house where she would soon dwell. Legacy's boyfriend Kane followed closely behind.

Shocked by her friend's presence, Tomorrow knelt behind her car hoping that her identity wouldn't be revealed.

"Why can't I spend the night like last time?" Legacy questioned as she was walked towards her car.

Kane remained silent and rudely pushed Legacy closer to her vehicle.

"Why are you pushing me? I can walk by myself!"

"We been through this a thousand times already." Kane argued. "I have an early class in the morning and I need to get some rest! Now get in your car and call me when you get home so that I know you made it safe."

Kane opened Legacy's door and waited for her to jump in. She hesitantly eased closer to her car but came to an abrupt halt when she noticed him checking his cell phone.

"Hold the fuck up! Who you fucking? What's that bitch's name?" Legacy shouted.

She poked Kane in the forehead with her index finger demanding an answer.

"Touch me one more time, Legacy, and I swear I will lay your ass out! You been gettin' too comfortable with that hittin' shit. Do it again, I dare you!"

"And I told you to keep your fucking voice down!" he said.

Kane smacked Legacy's hand down and looked from side to side. He hoped that his nosey neighbors weren't peeking from the windows. The last thing he needed was another

2

complaint about all of the commotion.

In the midst of arguing with Legacy, Kane couldn't help but notice Tomorrow's shiny black BMW parked directly across the street.

Without another word, he pushed Legacy into her car. He had to get her away from his house before she spotted Tomorrow's car.

He immediately shut the car door and leaned in.

"Look here, you said you was on your period anyway so it ain't like we was gon' fuck tonight. And you already said you don't feel like sucking my dick, so what is there left to do? You know I don't get down and wit' allat cuddle shit. So you can get mad if you want to but all I wanna do tonight is get my nut off and go to bed. So I will see you in the morning when you pick me up for class. Aight?"

Kane glanced through Legacy's passenger window and instantly noticed Tomorrow. He was nervous but he knew that if he was going to get away with cheating, he would have to remain calm.

Still in a rage, Legacy fired up her 1980 Buick Skylark. She sat and waited for the ticking sound in the engine to disappear and refused to look at Kane. She was tired of his constant wishy- washy behavior; all she really wanted was for him to treat her with some respect.

"Ok," Legacy uttered sadly before she finally drove off.

Tomorrow couldn't help but laugh at the scene. She was in utter disbelief at how Kane had thrown his girlfriend out of the house like she was nothing more than a cheap trick.

"Wow!" Tomorrow whispered.

She shook her head and pulled the last hit off of her blunt. She waited a few moments just to make sure the coast was clear. Once she was sure Legacy would not return, Tomorrow stood and threw her roach blunt on the ground. She popped the trunk and tossed in her empty bottle of Hennessy. After one last coast check, she grabbed her overnight bag and strutted across the street.

Kane admired her 5'9", 175-pound dark brown frame as she walked over to him. She was just enough woman for his tall, thick, football – player frame.

Tomorrow was built like what some would call an amazon woman. She had long, thick legs and a set of perky breasts that would put any stripper to shame.

She was a natural beauty with long flowing dark locs, full lips and big, bright brown eyes that could capture any man's heart. She exuded sensuality, which made her calm demeanor ooze with unadulterated sexiness.

Tomorrow had a girl next door persona with a wicked sex kitten alter ego that drove men crazy. She definitely wasn't the norm and Kane loved that about her.

"Here comes the pussy I've been feenin' for all night!" he thought to himself.

Without a word, he took her by the hand and guided her into his house. The two kissed all the way downstairs until they reached his bedroom in the basement.

"Man, I thought we were busted." Tomorrow laughed carelessly.

"I know right. But shit, I ain't worried about it. That bitch is sprung off my dick."

"Why was she even here? You know damn well we get it in every Thursday night!"

Kane and Tomorrow sat down at the foot of his king size bed.

"That broad is psycho! I broke up with her last night on the phone and her ass still stopped by acting like nothing ever happened."

"Whatever! You know that's your boo. She's been on

your dick ever since the eighth grade," Tomorrow teased. "You know what? I honestly believe that she only started fucking with you because she knew that Mishon was checkin' for you."

"Wait! Mishon liked me for real? She mad cute. But I thought she was fucking with that nigga Brandon from New York."

"Yeah, they still talk. She don't want your ass no more. You're old news now, nigga. It's been like six years," Tomorrow said blatantly.

Kane looked at Tomorrow with a pitiful but slightly intrigued expression. He couldn't believe that she was so bold. Tomorrow always spoke with such conviction and never had any reservations about saying exactly what was on her mind.

Kane despised when Legacy spoke her mind. He could barely stand listening to her for longer than five minutes before he completely blanked out, but hearing Tomorrow spit her truths was a complete turn on.

"I don't mean to be rude or nothing like that, but dude, don't you know that everybody on campus is straight laughing at your ass?" she continued.

Her brown and blunt combo had her feeling quite lovely. At that point, she honestly couldn't care less what slipped from her mouth.

Kane gave Tomorrow a confused look.

"But why?" he asked.

"Because your girl be walking around like she got a leash around your fucking neck, when in reality, that bitch the one who need a leash."

"Why you goin' in? I thought that was your girl. Y'all seem like best friends when we in class."

"Boy, blah." Tomorrow laughed. "Everybody say you a punk ass nigga for letting her get over like that. And you let bitch stalk you too?"

Tomorrow shook her head in disgust.

"Just keeping it real," Kane said, "I don't give a shit what anybody has to say about me. I'm only fucking with her cuz the bitch got a whip and she keep my pockets right. It's not that serious."

Kane took his shirt off and flopped back onto the bed with his hands behind his head. Tomorrow watched as he revealed his fit physique and she casually fell into her own personal exotic daydream.

Tomorrow viewed Kane as nothing more than a sexual play toy. In fact, she really thought he was quite lame and initially only slept with him as a spiteful attempt to betray her so-called friend Legacy.

Tomorrow couldn't stand Legacy, mostly due to the fact that Legacy didn't want her anywhere near their best friend Mishon. She knew that Legacy hated her, so she found pleasure in sleeping with her man just for the hell of it. But once she actually had a taste of Kane, she realized that she'd have to keep him around for her own personal pleasure.

Kane may have been lame, but what he lacked in personality, he made up for in the bedroom. His aggressive, take charge attitude during sex caught Tomorrow completely off guard. She had expected lackluster sex that she'd live to regret. Fortunately, she was pleasantly surprised, and after their first encounter, she made up her mind that she'd enjoy more of his mind blowing sex, even if that meant she'd be getting sloppy seconds.

Kane wasn't Tomorrow's type by any means. Tomorrow liked guys who had take-charge and in-control personalities; yet, Kane was generally quite the opposite. He allowed people to run all over him, especially Legacy.

Kane grew up as the local fat kid, so for most of his life, he was either made fun of or completely ignored. However, after puberty hit, he got into sports and the baby fat rapidly turned to muscle. With the muscle, of course came girls, and with girls came his newfound self esteem. The problem was he was still socially awkward.

Kane wasn't a thug. He was simply a normal dude who wanted to be accepted. He was cheesy and inauthentic, but he tried his best to fit in. It just never quite seemed to work out for him.

"If you say so." Tomorrow shrugged. "Well, enough about that silly ho! It's after midnight and I really didn't come here to talk."

Tomorrow casually got on her knees and crawled to the middle of Kane's bed. She raised her tight fitted dress over her head and revealed her black, rhinestone draped g-string.

"I came to ride that fat, nine inch dick," Tomorrow said seductively.

Kane bit his bottom lip and grabbed the bulge in his shorts. He was ready to give Tomorrow just what she came for.

"Well let's cut to the chase then."

Kane pulled out his dick. He showed just enough without fully pulling his basketball shorts down. "I'm ready to be served. Oh and don't worry, you will be equally if not more satisfied before the night is over." Kane softly spoke.

They began a slow and passionate kiss. Tomorrow followed their normal routine and slowly nibbled on Kane's ear. He immediately felt his dick get hard and he couldn't resist. He wanted to feel the sensation of her warm wet lips on all nine inches of his thickness.

Kane forcefully pushed Tomorrow's head down until her eyes met his dick. He knew she liked that rough and kinky shit and would have no problem indulging.

She greedily sucked his dick like a professional porno star, looking up at him every so often to make sure he was in utter ecstasy.

"Damn girl, you be givin' that fire head! That's right, suck it! Put all that dick in your mouth!"

Tomorrow sucked on the tip of Kane's dick like she was devouring a Blow Pop. The overwhelming sensation turned his body stiff and caused his eyes to roll in the back of his head.

Kane couldn't take it anymore. The pleasure was too intense and it caused his body to go numb. He was speechless. He knew that if she kept that up, she would have a mouth full of his cum.

"I see you can barely talk now," Tomorrow teased. "How 'bout I get on top and ride this dick for a while? Would you like that?"

Kane nodded in agreement. No words escaped, but his mouth remained wide open. He was in shock at how talented she was. Tomorrow seemed like such a good girl and yet she was about to fuck his brains out like she was a champion.

Tomorrow jumped on top of Kane and began riding hard, squeezing her pussy muscles tightly, and giving him no chance to rest between the strokes. Kane grabbed her by the waist to help bring each stroke in harder. Tomorrow moaned in delight. Kane had some great dick and she was enjoying every moment.

"Lay the fuck down! I'm ready to eat some pussy now."

Kane forcefully flipped her over and in one pull, ripped off what was left of her dress and threw it on the floor.

He spread her legs and pulled his shorts all the way down to his knee caps. Tomorrow slowly pulled her g-string to the side and played with her protruding clit. Kane yanked the g-string out of her hand and went face deep into her pussy. He slowly licked her pearl, dragging his tongue gently across both lips.

"Ooooh!" Tomorrow moaned, pinching her nipples,

creating a stinging sensation.

Kane inserted his index and middle finger into her pussy while he tongued her down. Looking at her facial expressions only made him want her that much more.

He could feel his dick dripping pre-cum and he knew he was ready to feel the tightness and wetness of her sweet, juicy pussy again. He wanted to make sure she was ready for all nine inches. He continued to finger her pussy while he circled her clit with his tongue. The deeper he inserted his fingers, the louder she became.

"Just like that," she moaned.

Kane pushed Tomorrow onto her side, licking her from front to back. Just when she thought she was headed to complete ecstasy, Kane's cell phone rang.

"Man, fuck!" He shrieked looking for his phone.

Tomorrow sat up and wrapped her sweaty body in Kane's bed sheet. She knew exactly who was calling his phone, and quite frankly, she was pissed. It was bad enough that she already had to wait to be fucked because of Kane's negligence, but now he had managed to completely ruin her nut.

"It ain't nobody but Legacy. How much you wanna bet?"

Kane found his phone on the dresser, but he didn't answer it in time. He checked the missed call log on his phone.

"Yep, it was her. And now she's leaving me a text."

"What's it say?"

Kane frantically checked his inbox message.

"Oh shit! She at the front door."

"Why?"

Tomorrow rolled her eyes. She didn't have time for Kane and Legacy's antics. She could be getting dicked down by a dude twice his age whose dick game was on point and one who wouldn't have any interruptions.

9

"Man, I don't know! The text just said that she's been knocking on the front door for about five minutes now.

"Then go upstairs and answer the door."

Kane sighed and pulled up his shorts.

"You gotta be joking. My dick still hard and you want me to open the door like this? Look at it. You can see it sticking out of my shorts!"

Tomorrow really didn't give a damn about what Kane chose to do. She walked over to her overnight bag and found the rest of her stash. It was definitely time to roll up another blunt.

"If I answer the door, she's going to wanna come in!"

"Well, you're gonna have to think quickly. Tell that bitch to beat it or something. All I know is if you don't go up and get the door, she is gonna be suspicious. And if she keeps it up, your mother gonna answer it, and it's almost two in the morning."

Kane didn't want to open the door but he knew Tomorrow was right. He scrambled around the dark room until he found a shirt to hide the scratch marks on his back.

"Do you think she saw your car?" Kane asked nervously. "Why would you even park your car on the other side of the street anyway?" He continued without allowing Tomorrow to answer.

He threw his hands in the air, afraid that Legacy had finally caught him cheating.

"Because I don't give a fuck! That's your bitch and it aint got shit to do with me…I'm just here for the dick."

Tomorrow emptied her blunt guts in the trash can next to the bed.

"You got a taste of this pussy for the last forty-five minutes and now because your flunky here, you want to act brand new?"

Tomorrow grabbed her overnight bag and prepared to leave.

"Nigga, fuck you. I don't need this shit!" She yelled.

"Slow down! Let me handle this. Smoke your blunt and chill out. I will be back shortly," Kane declared.

He raced upstairs hoping his mom didn't already invite Legacy in. When he made it to the living room, he saw that she was still standing outside of the door. He watched as she looked through the door's mail slot, but it was too dark for her to see anything inside. She knocked again.

Finally, he opened the door and stepped outside. He stretched his arms and yawned. He figured he'd just tell Legacy that he was asleep.

Legacy hugged him and began to whine.

"What are you doing here? Don't you know what time it is?"

"I had nowhere else to go. I was supposed to stay over Mishon's house but she's not home."

"Why didn't you go home?"

"My mother has her boyfriend over tonight and there's not enough room for me to sleep there. You know it's only a one-bedroom apartment."

Kane rolled his eyes. *This bitch is fucking shit up right now,* he thought to himself.

"It's true! Call my mother yourself."

"Look, I don't know what else to tell you but you can't stay here tonight."

"What?"

"Why don't you call Mishon's parents and see if they will let you in?"

Legacy grew furious. She didn't understand why Kane had such an attitude. She had stayed at his house plenty of times before, and now, all of a sudden he didn't want her there?

11

"So where am I gonna go Kane?" Legacy screamed.

"Aye, you need to pipe the fuck down. I got neighbors and shit. Plus, my moms in here and she prolly sleep. Man, gimme a sec."

Kane wasn't sure of what to do, but he knew he just couldn't leave Legacy hanging. Although he wasn't in love with her, there was a part of him that really cared about her, and besides, she had the ride.

He went back down to his bedroom to tell Tomorrow that they would have to cut their session short, but she was already gone.

Damn! he thought aloud.

Kane's phone buzzed on the dresser. He figured it was just Legacy calling him again. He grabbed the phone and noticed that the text was from Tomorrow:

Next Thursday make sure there's no fatal attraction :)

Kane laughed to himself. There was definitely something about Tomorrow that he just couldn't shake. And most of all, he was glad that she was quick on her toes. She had snuck out the back door without him even asking.

He sprayed some Febreeze on his sheets and ran back upstairs to let Legacy in.

"What the fuck took so damn long?"

"I had to make sure my moms was sleep," Kane lied.

"You never had to do that before."

"Yeah, well she been tripping lately cuz Trell and them be here mad late making noise and shit. So I just don't want no issues."

"I don't know why you hang with Trell and Dee anyway. They not on your level, baby. I've been told you 'bout them fools."

"Yeah, whatever. Come on in and excuse the room. I

wasn't expecting company."

Kane searched the room with his eyes to make sure that Tomorrow hadn't left anything behind.

Everything looked good. Legacy sat on the bed and took off her shoes. He hopped back into bed and got underneath his covers.

"Damn, you're just gonna go to sleep?"

Legacy was disappointed. She wanted Kane to at least pretend that he was happy she was there with him.

"For the lasssst time, I told you I have shit to do tomorrow, so get some rest."

"Ugh, I can't stand you sometimes," Legacy sighed before she joined him in the bed.

Trust me bitch, right now that feeling is definitely mutual.

***

Tomorrow laughed as she sent Kane the text from her car. She couldn't believe how everything had gone down. She was so over being with young dudes who didn't know how to handle their shit. Kane's sex game was on point, but the fact that he didn't have his bitch in check was a major turn off. Since she had ditched Kane, she thought it was only right to let a real man finish the job.

She scrolled through her phone and saw Mike's name. At first, she was reluctant to call because of the history she shared with Mike. Being with him could cause all types of unnecessary drama, but that made her want him even more. The bad things that could happen if anyone found out about Mike were limitless, and yet, Tomorrow simply didn't care.

She sent him a text message to let him know that she was on the way and then headed to the other side of town. Because her car was easily detectable in this particular neighborhood, she decided against parking on the street.

Instead, she parked inside of the parking garage diagonal to his apartment building, a spot that held a lot of cars so there was no way anyone would spot hers.

Tomorrow had slipped into Kane's bathroom and took a hoe bath before she left, but she wanted to freshen up a bit more. She went into her overnight bag and pulled out her feminine wipes, feminine spray and a new little sexy outfit.

Before exiting the car, she sparked one last blunt. She noticed her phone vibrating and saw that Mike was texting her:

Everything is good, come on up. Make sure you use that door pass I gave you to get in on the side of the building.

That was her cue. She pulled out her pass and headed across the street to his apartment building. Once she reached his door, she knocked twice and waited for him to open up.

"Damn, you're looking sexy as hell in that. All this for me?"

A tall, dark chocolate, muscular man stood at the door admiring Tomorrow's body.

"Of course, daddy, who else would it be for?"

"Mmm, you know I love it when you call me daddy. Get your sexy ass in here!"

Tomorrow walked into his lavish apartment admiring the familiar surroundings. Family pictures hung on the rose colored walls, obviously a woman's touch.

"I haven't heard from you in a few days, Mike. You forgot how good this pussy is?" Tomorrow joked.

"Never. I've just been busy, you know how it goes. Plus, I'm a family man so it's hard to be alone sometimes."

Mike was practically a married man. He had never signed any papers but he and his longtime girlfriend had been shacking up for years. Mike was an older man, nearly in his forties, and knew that sex with an eighteen-year-old was wrong, no matter how fine she was, but he just couldn't resist Tomorrow's charm.

From the first time he saw her, he knew that he wanted her badly. He made no reservations about just how much he had to have her. She was like a drug to him, and like a fiend, Mike was seeking his next hit.

"Get naked!" Tomorrow demanded. "I want you to fuck me right here by the door, daddy."

"Damn, you always know exactly what to say don't you?" Mike grinned.

"Yes indeed."

By the end of the night, Tomorrow had been fucked and sucked just the way she had hoped, free of interruptions. She managed to leave a smile on Mike's face and slid away before his girlfriend Flo came home from work.

In less than five hours, Tomorrow had to be up and ready for class. But what the hell, it was Friday.

CHAPTER

~ 2 ~

All of the students of D. C. University College were happy that the weekend had finally come. Mid-terms were over and Spring Break was approaching.

Kane had a full schedule of classes for the day and had done his best to avoid seeing Legacy. Even in the classes they shared, it was very apparent that he had nothing to say to her.

Legacy tried her best to get Kane's attention but he barely even looked in her direction. She didn't get why he was so upset, but she had the sneaking suspicion that he was messing around.

During a break between classes, she was fed up and needed to talk to her girls about what was going on. They sat down at their favorite table in the university's courtyard. Mishon pulled out the McDonald's that she got during one of her breaks.

"Y'all will not believe what is going on right now," Legacy said.

Tomorrow and Mishon rolled their eyes. They knew that this story was going to be outlandish at best. Legacy was so dramatic and no one really took her seriously, not even her own friends.

"What happened now?" Tomorrow said flatly.

"Kane had me waiting outside for like twenty minutes last night. It was raining and everything and he just acted like he didn't give a fuck."

"Bitch, is that it?" Mishon laughed. "I thought you were gonna say that the nigga punched you in the face or gave you crabs or something." Mishon and Tomorrow giggled at the thought.

"Listen, I think this nigga is fucking somebody else, cuz he was texting somebody and he acted like he wasn't gonna let me in the damn house. Twenty minutes outside!"

"Chick, do you have some concrete evidence of the cheating?" Mishon asked before sipping her Mountain Dew.

"No, but I can feel it. Once I find that shit out, it's a wrap! Y'all already know what time it is!" Legacy snapped.

"I done told y'all 'bout messing with these good-for-nothing niggas. You should be focusing on graduating, not being up in some nigga's face," Tomorrow chimed in.

"Bitch, shut up, we can't all be perfect like you," Legacy said.

"Whatever, I'm just trying to help you out. True love waits," Tomorrow said, shaking the celibacy band that she got from a church retreat in front of Legacy's face.

Mishon shot Tomorrow a sarcastic look and they

shared a laugh as they chomped on their McDonald's fries. Legacy was too self absorbed to notice that the girls were having a laugh at her expense.

The girls had known each other for years. They all grew up in Alexandria, Virginia, which was a small city right outside of Washington, D.C. After high school graduation, the girls decided that it was best to stay in the area and go to a small, private, and local University.

They all chose DCUC as their university of choice. With their good grades, Tomorrow and Mishon received full scholarships, and Legacy simply followed along.

Mishon and Tomorrow were best friends. They had met in the ninth grade, and after having nearly every class together, the two became inseparable. Although Mishon had known Legacy a year before she met Tomorrow, they were never as close.

They all had strong personalities that didn't always mesh, but they somehow managed to put up with each other.

Legacy could be a cool person, but she was so misunderstood. Her bubbly and clingy personality was sometimes overwhelming, and she didn't know how to bring it down from a level ten to a level two. Because of that, along with the annoyingly whiny baby voice that she spoke in so often, people simply didn't want to be bothered. Legacy was the type of person who struggled to make friends, and once she made them, she struggled even harder to keep them.

Throughout the four years that the girls had known each other, Legacy was the tag-along that Mishon and Tomorrow just put up with. Although she looked to Mishon as her saving grace, both girls had to equally endure her irritating ways.

Mishon was a free spirit. Because her mother worked all the time and her mother's boyfriend couldn't stand her, she basically had to raise herself. She was naturally feisty and flirtatious and was always down for a good time. No one ever understood how these three girls became so close because they appeared to be so different.

Although no one would ever guess it, Mishon and Tomorrow were one in the same.

To the world, Tomorrow appeared to be an intelligent, overachieving, do-gooder bound for success. She was indeed all of those things, but she had an alter ego that was out of this world and made Mishon's wild ways look like child's play in comparison.

Tomorrow kept a relatively low profile and always did her dirt quietly and undetected. Mishon was one of the few people who she opened up to and it made their bond nearly unbreakable. Unfortunately, her secret lifestyle had dangerous consequences and once revealed, could ultimately ruin the lives of everyone around her.

"So Kane sent me a text earlier this morning in African American Lit. telling me that Trell is having a party tonight," Mishon informed the girls. "I think his mom is supposed to be out of town for the weekend. Did you get word Tomorrow?"

"Yeah, I saw Trell's cousin Dee at the corner store a couple of days ago. You know that party gonna be off the chain cuz them niggas live on the south side where the police don't give a damn." Tomorrow said.

Legacy couldn't believe what she was hearing.

"Wait! Why would Kane tell you about the party first when I was just over his house last night and he didn't tell me?" Legacy snapped.

Mishon and Tomorrow pretended to be in shock but they both knew the real reason that Kane or no one else mentioned the party to Legacy: nobody wanted her there.

"Why are you tripping so hard?" Mishon asked. "He

probably didn't tell you cuz it's not your type of party. I'm just sayin'." Mishon shrugged.

"What the fuck do you mean not my type of party? What about Tomorrow? Miss prissy got invited to the party and not me?"

"Don't trip. Ho, I'm fly, that's why I got an invite," Tomorrow defended herself.

"What's Tomorrow got to do with you being invited? You don't even like Trell and Dee anyway," Mishon added.

"I can get down just like you bitches but I choose not to because I already have my man. I ain't out here fucking every Tom, Dick and Harry."

"Now hold up, Legacy!" Mishon caught an attitude.

Tomorrow started to bite her Big Mack, but placed it back on her napkin once Legacy became a little rowdy. She found it funny that Legacy even considered Kane her man when he obviously had no intentions of being with her anymore.

"Nah, don't say nothing, Shon. I got this," Tomorrow interrupted. "First of all, I don't need to sleep with anyone to be accepted. I'm fly by blood, so get your facts straight, bitch! And even if I was fucking Tom, Dick or yo damn daddy, how the fuck would you know? I don't even really talk to you anymore," she continued.

"Tsk, and I know you ain't got nothing on me, bitch!" Mishon jumped back in.

Tomorrow wanted to really give Legacy a piece of her mind, but she knew that saying too much wouldn't be good. She needed to keep her own shit under wraps. The urge to be an asshole was just too overwhelming for her. She could have easily revealed that she was sleeping with Kane but she decided against it. Besides, she had other plans for that information.

When Mishon chimed in, Tomorrow went back to

enjoying her sandwich. She decided that instead of saying something slick, she'd just sit back and enjoy the show.

"But everybody knows your dirty little secrets," Mishon snapped. "Don't forget how you let that dude back in the eighth grade fuck you using a ripped piece of plastic bag he found in your kitchen."

Legacy gasped. She couldn't believe that her best friend was spreading her business, especially in front of someone that she hated.

Mishon continued to speak. She was unaffected by the stunned look on Legacy's face and continued to spew her business with no remorse.

"How lazy can you get? A box of condoms only cost what? Five bucks! Don't even fucking go there with me, cuz I will light your ass up in this courtyard."

Everyone grew silent. Inside, Tomorrow was laughing hysterically. She loved when Mishon put Legacy in her place. It made her feel all warm and fuzzy inside knowing that she had managed to snatch Legacy's best friend away without a second thought.

"Just calm down." Tomorrow pretended to be concerned.

"Nah, she needs to hear this! If I was Kane, I would be cheatin' on yo ass too. It's your mouf! You just let anything roll out of that muthafucka! But don't try that mess wit me, boo boo. You know betta than that shit."

Legacy pretended to be dumbfounded by what Mishon described. In fact, she remembered the incident quite well and couldn't believe that her best friend would bring it back up when they had promised never to speak of it again. Her eyes welled with tears but she wouldn't say another word.

Damn, is that all we had to do to get this bitch to shut the fuck up? Tomorrow thought.

22

Legacy remained quiet for the remainder of their break. She felt remorseful about snapping off on the girls. It wasn't their fault that Kane hadn't invited her to the party anyway.

"In other news, bitch did you watch Fox 5 last night?" Mishon changed the subject.

"Nah, what happened?" Tomorrow joined in.

"How about that bitch Kiss of Death done struck again. It was some dude in Georgetown. He was a professor at Howard, fine as hell."

"Kiss of Death?" Tomorrow asked, confused.

"Yeah bitch, you know, the Lipstick Serial Killer! You ain't up on that shit? There's a fucking psycho bitch killing all the sexy niggas in the DMV. I swear this bitch is gangsta as shit. She fuck the niggas, then kill 'em," Mishon raved.

"Word? I heard about that, but I ain't know that's what they were calling her."

"Hell yeah. That's her name cuz she leaves her kiss print on their fucking foreheads. That bitch has got to get a LMN movie deal. I just know it!"

Mishon seemed a bit overly excited about a mass murder that was going on so close to home, but Tomorrow didn't seem concerned enough.

"That shit is crazy," Mishon continued.

"Hell yeah, but anyway, let's go. I got a one o'clock class. Bye Legacy, we'll catch you later," Tomorrow teased.

"Uh huh," Legacy replied.

Mishon and Tomorrow walked out the courtyard and headed to their next class. They left Legacy behind in the crowd.

"Can you believe that trick?" Mishon laughed. "I bet she will think twice about what comes out of her mouth now."

"I don't think so," Tomorrow disagreed. "You know how she is. One day she's pissed off at nothing and then the next, she acts like we been besties for years. Anyway, what class do you have next? I have Human Sexuality."

Tomorrow was a Psychology major with a minor in Journalism. She loved learning about the mind and how it worked, and she definitely loved writing about it.

"Ugh, I got Biology," Mishon responded. "But I'm about to skip for the rest of the day. Besides, I need to hit up the mall to find something to wear for tonight. Are you coming with?"

Tomorrow thought it was a good Idea, especially since she didn't get any sleep the night before.

"Damn, I love that class, but I guess I can miss one. Meet me at my house in about twenty-five minutes.

"That's what's up, make it more like forty-five minutes, cuz I need to holla at Brandon real quick. Plus, I'mma run home and grab a few things. Might as well get ready over your house tonight."

Mishon searched the hallways in the west wing of the Sharpton-Rose building hoping to run across Brandon. She wanted to tell him her plans for the night, but there was no sign of him.

"I guess I'll just see him later on tonight," She mumbled to herself before she headed for the door.

Mishon made way to her bright new red 2009 Toyota Camry, courtesy of her boyfriend's new gig.

She smiled as she opened the door. Things were finally looking up for her. Life was good and she was definitely reaping the benefits of being with a dude like Brandon. But there was one thing that stood in the way of her complete happiness, and that one thing was her home life.

She dreaded going home. She and her generic stepfather were always at odds, which often caused her to stay away from the apartment.

Sometimes he would piss Mishon off intentionally just

so she could storm out of the house and he could do whatever it was that he did when she was away. Mishon didn't have proof, but she knew that her mom's boyfriend was up to no good.

Her mother worked crazy hours at Reagan National Airport and therefore, had no time to rectify the issues between her man and her daughter. Eventually, Mishon just decided to cut all ties from them both. While she physically still lived there with them, she did everything she could to separate herself from the foolishness that went on in her household.

Mishon pulled up to her apartment garage and searched for a vacant parking spot. Once she parked, she decided to call her mother just to let her know that she'd probably stay out all night again, but there was no answer. She headed for her apartment, thinking of the things she wanted to grab before she walked through the door. Mishon wanted this trip to be short and sweet.

She inserted her key into the keyhole and walked in. Mishon hoped that he wouldn't be there, but unfortunately, of course, he was. She saw him lying on the couch smoking a cigarette and watching Maury.

What a fucking bum, Mishon thought to herself.

"I see you decided to come home today," he said.

When Mishon didn't respond, he sat up and repeated himself in a firm tone.

"I said…I see you decided to come home today."

Mishon stood at the front door and rolled her eyes.

"What do you care? I'm grown," she sassed.

"How 'bout I call your mom and see what she has to say about it?"

"Yeah, good luck with that one, asshole," Mishon uttered.

She dropped her book bag by the door and headed to her bedroom. Her mom's boyfriend became infuriated by her sarcastic attitude. He jumped off the sofa, pulled the last hit off his Newport and followed her down the hallway.

He couldn't stand the fact that Mishon always had the upper hand. No matter what she did or how many times he threatened to tell her mother, he knew she would always get away with it. Because of that very fact, he wanted to make her life a living nightmare. He couldn't stand her rude and defiant ways and let her know that every chance he got.

"Oh, I get it now!" he yelled with wide eyes.

You could see the veins popping out the side of his neck. He had Mishon right where he wanted her.

"You still mad about last night when I threw your smart ass out the house, huh?" he smirked.

"Nigga, please."

"Who the fuck are you talking to, little girl? Don't make me kirk the fuck out! You don't run shit up in here! Thinking you grown and shit!"

He finally made his way to her bedroom and stood inside the doorway. He watched as Mishon grabbed everything she needed and threw it in one big pile on her bed. She continued to ignore his antics.

"I don't know why you grabbing shit out your closet 'cause you ain't going nowhere. Your ass ain't going nowhere until you start giving me the respect I deserve for being the man of this house!"

Angrily, he kicked her door and watched it fly back into the wall. Mishon dug into her pockets and grabbed her cell phone. She quickly put it on the dresser just in case he tried to get physical like he had done the night before.

"What you gonna do? Call the cops on me?" He laughed. "Or better yet, why don't you call Brandon again and see what happens to him. Tell that nigga to leave his goons behind this time and walk up in here and swing on me. Had

26

that punk motherfucker and his boys jump me! Because of yo' trifling ass!"

Mishon stuffed her belongings into her travel bag in a hurry. Some of her things hung out of the side, but she didn't care. She attempted to rush out of her bedroom door. Mishon fiercely pushed into his stomach but he didn't budge.

"Nigga, move!" she ordered.

"Make me!" he taunted.

He shot her an evil glare.

Mishon walked up really close to him and stared him dead in face. She was so close that she could see her own reflection in his eyes.

"Or how about I call Mom and tell her about that skeleton you got hanging in your closet?" Mishon whispered. "I mean, it's really none of my business, but I wouldn't mind telling her."

Mishon smiled and stood there waiting for his response.

His mouth began to get dry and his heart pounded profusely. He wasn't exactly sure what Mishon was speaking about because he had so many secrets. He knew deep down that he was a fucked up nigga only in it for himself.

He was an ex con with no job and didn't plan on finding one. But what he did have was sex appeal and charm; he knew he was sexy and always used it to his advantage.

Five years before, he had met Mishon's mom while traveling on what he liked to call a "business" trip. He wined and dined her and before Mishon even had the chance to protest, he was living off of her mother, rent free.

He eventually asked for her hand in marriage, but everybody knew that a wedding would never happen. It was all a part of his plan. He stayed with her, not because he loved her, but for security.

Mishon's mother was a hard worker and maintained

nice things. He wanted to be a part of that. What he hadn't bargained for was her loud mouthed, out of control teenage daughter.

Without any words, he slid aside to let Mishon pass. He stared at her with an intense glare as she walked by wearing that same vindictive smile.

"Skanky bitch!" he said quietly as she switched down the hallway carrying her bag.

As soon as Mishon walked out the door, she burst into laughter.

Gee this nigga really believed me. I need to become an actress.

She threw her bag in the back seat of her car, put on her Gucci shades and pulled off. She tried calling her mom's cell again but there was still no answer.

Mishon looked down at her phone and realized that her run-in with her mom's dude had put her way behind schedule. She sped to Tomorrow's house and prayed that she wouldn't get pulled over for speeding.

"Fuck, I'm late!"

Mishon tried to send a text and drive at the same time, but Brandon called and interrupted the message.

"Hello?"

"Hey Miss Lady, I see you left school early today. Am I going to see you at the party tonight?" Brandon asked.

"Yea, I'mma be there around ten. I'm headed to my girl Tomorrow's house, and from there we gon' head to the party."

"Aight, well we can link up for a lil' bit afterwards. I got sum shit to take care of tonight."

"Can we just get a hotel room like we did last night?"

"I guess so. Something went down, huh? What happened at home now?"

"Nothing serious. I will tell you when I see you tonight."

Mishon didn't want to say too much, especially because she knew that Brandon would go crazy if he even thought that her "stepdad" was tripping again.

"If you say so. Talk to you later, love."

"Bye."

"Damn bitch, 'bout time you got here. What took you so long?" Tomorrow asked as she opened the door to let Mishon in.

"Bitch, mayday! This nigga done lost it at the house. He is so fucking wack, I don't even know why my mom is still with that fake Taye Diggs looking ass nigga anyway."

Mishon walked inside of Tomorrow's townhome. She couldn't help but admire the house as she walked towards Tomorrow's room. It was so elegantly decorated, and every time she visited, she never wanted to leave.

But it wasn't just the decor that had Mishon mesmerized. There was a sense of peace whenever she entered the house, something that she rarely experienced at home.

"Girl, leave that man alone. You always going in on him. He do look like a Taye Diggs knock off though!" Tomorrow laughed.

"Yeah, a broke, conniving, junky ass version," Mishon added. "He better have some good ass sex for all the shit that my mom puts up with. That would be the least that nigga could do," she continued.

"Hmm," Tomorrow replied. "So you ready to hit the mall or not?" She changed the subject.

"Yeah, let's hurry up and go so we can get back."

CHAPTER

~ 3 ~

*L*egacy sat on her bed wondering why she hadn't heard from Mishon, Tomorrow, or even Kane for that matter. She got word from another classmate who spotted Mishon and Tomorrow at the mall.

"They must be trying to get ready for that party tonight," she said aloud.

Legacy knew that there was no way she was going to miss that party. She figured that Kane would never expect her to be there, and because of that, she was determined to go. She just knew that she would catch him cheating.

It was true, Legacy initially only wanted to date Kane after she found out that Mishon liked him. She secretly wanted to be just like her and was jealous that Mishon didn't have to do much to get attention.

Mishon had a beautiful light skinned complexion that looked as if it was slightly kissed by the sun. At 5'4" and 130 pounds, she caught the eyes of many.

Legacy was a nice mix of Caribbean flavors. She was chocolate brown, 5'5" and 135 pounds. While Legacy was beautiful in her own right, she always compared herself to Mishon. There was really only one thing that Mishon had that Legacy didn't, and that was true self confidence.

By beating Mishon to the punch and getting Kane's attention, Legacy felt like she had one up on her friend. But now, she really liked Kane. Hell, she even loved him, and the fact that his love wasn't reciprocated made her crazy. She knew that she had to do something to get him to stay with her forever. She just didn't know what that something was just yet.

"Hey Mishon, where you at?" Legacy asked, hearing Bob Marley blaring in the background.

She figured that Mishon was just somewhere getting high.

"I'm at Tomorrow's spot getting dressed. We 'bout to head to the party. Why, what's up?"

Mishon already knew what was coming. Legacy always did this. If she knew that Tomorrow and Mishon were together, she'd always beg to be the tag-along.

"I wanna go to the party. Can y'all come pick me up? I can be ready in like 30 minutes."

"Look, I'm tryna enjoy this blunt right now," Mishon replied.

"You can still come get me. By the time you get finished, I'll be ready," Legacy insisted.

This bitch just won't give up. "Aight, chick." Mishon sighed. "Just be ready by the time I get there. I'm honking two times. If you don't run out, I'm gone."

"Bitch, don't be acting like you don't want me to come, it's not that serious. I just said I'll be ready."

"Watch your tone, bitch, just make sure you are."

"Bye."

The party was definitely jumping. The music blared from the DJ's speakers and you could hear it before you even reached the door. The girls hoped that the party wouldn't get shut down like the last one on the other side of town.

Mishon knocked on the door and Trell's older brother Quan answered. He licked his lips admiring how sexy the girls looked in their outfits.

"So are you just gonna stand there drooling, or are you gonna let us in?" Mishon said seductively.

"Come on in. Damn, y'all looking hella fine."

Quan stepped aside and allowed the girls into the house.

"Thank you," the girls said in unison.

The place was packed. Everybody who was anybody was definitely up in that basement.

The three girls stuck together for the beginning of the party but they knew it wouldn't be long before they were separated. They said their hellos to everyone that they knew and kept it moving.

Everyone was in shock when they saw Tomorrow walk through the door. She wasn't a typical partier, but after the week she just had, she needed a release.

People offered her smoke and drink, but she politely declined. She knew she had an image to maintain, so she made sure she played it cool. Besides, she and Mishon had gotten fucked up before they left her house, so she was feeling quite lovely.

As Tomorrow walked in Quan's direction, she noticed him staring at her with a seductive look. He looked her up and down before grabbing his dick. She wasn't sure if she should be turned on or offended by his gesture, but because she was a closet freak, she definitely got a little moist down below.

"Mmm," he said. "Damn girl, you are thick as hell. You got a man?"

Quan grabbed Tomorrow by the hand before she could walk by. Mishon and Legacy stopped and waited for her, but she quickly gave Mishon the secret signal to let her know that it was okay for them to keep walking.

"No, I'm single. And I like it that way."

She stepped so close to Quan that they were almost inhaling each other's breath. She knew that she had him hooked when he immediately got hard.

Tomorrow was a pro at reading dudes. She knew every trick of the trade and knew that Quan would be no different than the others.

"Oh, is that right? What's your name?"

"Tomorrow."

"Tomorrow. That's a pretty name. I've never seen you at none of these parties before."

"Yeah, it's my first time. I don't really do the party thing. Not really my scene."

"So why are you here?"

Quan was intrigued by Tomorrow. He sensed that she wasn't like other girls, and yet, she exuded this sexual energy that he couldn't escape. What was it about her that drove him crazy?

"Maybe for you."

Tomorrow leaned in even closer and softly nibbled on Quan's ear. He grabbed her ass and pulled her in closer. He wanted to fuck her right there in the middle of the party and he didn't care who watched.

"Aye, let's go somewhere," Quan whispered to her.

34

"Nah, I'm cooling tonight. Maybe another time."

"Damn ma, are you serious? You got me on swole right now. Why you playing?" Quan begged.

"Come dance with me."

Tomorrow smiled seductively and led Quan to a corner of the basement. She looked over and noticed that Mishon was already grinding on some dude and Legacy was dancing alone waiting for Kane to arrive.

Her favorite song, Jeremih's "Birthday Sex," blared through the speakers and she knew it was on. Tomorrow wound her hips in a slow groove making sure that her ass rubbed against the dick print in Quan's jeans. He grabbed her by the waist and pulled Tomorrow into him even more, causing some heavy friction between the two. She could feel him protruding and it was turning her on.

"Damn, girl."

That was the only thing that Quan managed to say. The intensity from the dance had them both wanting to burst. Before they knew it, they had danced together nearly the entire night. He didn't want to let her go.

When she noticed Mishon coming towards her, she could tell that the party was officially over. Mishon had a worried look on her face and Tomorrow knew that shit was about to get real.

"Girl...Mayday! I don't know what the fuck is up, but Brandon is up in here tripping. Let's go!"

"Why, what is he doing?"

Tomorrow was annoyed. She had planned to put Quan on her list of fuck buddies, but Mishon was cock blocking.

"He keep asking me shit about Kane. I don't know where the fuck this shit is coming from. Now he all like, Well I'mma ask him when he get here."

"What? Why would he be asking about Kane? I'm

confused."

"Bitch, you remember like six years ago when I said I liked Kane or whatever? But then Legacy started dating him and I was like, okay, fuck it? Well, apparently this nigga knows I liked him and started braggin' to his boys and shit. Then whoever he told obviously called up Brandon and fuck...I just don't need this shit right now."

Snitch ass nigga, Tomorrow thought to herself. I knew I shouldn't have said nothing to his punk ass. Let's see if he get any pussy from me now.

"That nigga is so lame. He really had the nerve to be spreading that around when he clearly is with Legacy?"

"Well, obviously he don't care about that cuz he's fucking you," Mishon sharply whispered.

Tomorrow shot Mishon a look that said, Bitch, don't say that shit while people are around.

"Okay, so where is Kane?" Tomorrow asked.

"He just fucking walked in and Legacy is all up in his grill, so now's the chance to exit this mutherfucka before shit get real," Mishon said in a rush.

Tomorrow looked back over at Quan where he was waiting patiently for her. She walked over to him and whispered something in his ear. He smiled, pulled out his phone and waited for Tomorrow to put in her number.

Once they exchanged contact info, Mishon grabbed Tomorrow by the arm and led her through the crowd. Before they could make their way back to the front, they heard a little commotion.

"Nigga, what's this shit I been hearing about you and my girl?" Brandon stepped to Kane.

Brandon was infuriated at the thought that somebody else was giving it to his girl. He had a lot invested in Mishon. They had been together for over a year and she knew things

36

about him that nobody else knew. He kept her laced and made sure she had the finer things in life.

Brandon was the product of a gangster and a dope fiend. His dad died before he was born, but he somehow managed to adopt a similar mentality. Unlike his father, Brandon wasn't the typical thug. Money was his motivation, but he made sure that any business venture that he was involved in, whether legal or illegal, worked out in his favor.

Brandon had an old soul. He was definitely wise beyond his years and it showed in the manner in which he carried himself. He was smooth, intelligent and very calculated with a calm demeanor but had a sharp temper that was not to be played with.

He was a dope boy, and although school was the last thing on his mind, he knew that with a degree, he couldn't be touched. Both street smarts and school smarts, what could be better than that? Besides, after he met Mishon, she encouraged him to stay in school, but not just because it was the right thing to do. She wanted him to look squeaky clean on the outside.

Brandon had money. It was simply his choice to follow in both is father's and his uncle's footsteps. His uncle Zeus, who was a big time drug lord in New York, left Brandon and his mother some property in D.C. along with some stow away cash that he put in trust funds before it could be detected by the feds. He wanted to make sure that Brandon and his mother were well taken care of while he was away. Zeus knew that his little sister's bad drug habit would eventually catch up to her and his young nephew would ultimately be the one who had to hold everything down. So before he went away, he taught Brandon everything he knew about the game and exactly how it was supposed to be played.

At 20, Brandon had seen and done some things that you only see in the movies. But he was smart about it. He lived lavishly, but not outlandishly. He made sure that every dime that he spent could be accounted for if shit ever went tumbling down.

He had seen a lot of things in his life that turned him into a very guarded person and the one thing he hated more than anything was feeling like somebody was getting over on him.

A few days before the party, Brandon's cousin Rico put him on about Kane running around campus saying that he could have Mishon if he wanted her. Although he wanted to put hands on Kane the second he heard the rumor, he decided that it was best he waited until this party to confront him.

Brandon loved Mishon, but he refused to allow her to play him. So for her sake, he hoped that Kane was just running his mouth, because he didn't want any harm to come to her.

He didn't plan on fighting Kane unless he absolutely had to, but he wasn't going to drop the situation.

"Dude. What the fuck are you talking about?" Kane turned around and looked Brandon dead in the eyes.

"Nigga, let me rephrase the muthafuckin' question. Are you fucking my girl?"

Brandon put one hand in his pocket letting Kane know that he wasn't joking around. Kane got a little nervous. He had only heard rumors about Brandon's lifestyle, but he wasn't sure if they were true. They hadn't really encountered each other before today.

"Maybe you should ask your girl," Kane snickered.

His pride wouldn't let him show any fear, even though he secretly hoped that Brandon wasn't carrying any heat.

"No nigga, I'm asking you. And my patience is wearing a little thin, so I suggest you answer the muthafuckin' question. I've been hearing you going around telling people you could steal my girl. So nigga, what's up? Where's that big shit you talking now nigga, huh?"

Mishon grabbed Tomorrow by the hand and they ran over to where Kane and Brandon stood.

"I'm not fucking this dude Brandon. I already told you that shit!" Mishon yelled.

"I'm asking him, not you." Brandon didn't even look at Mishon.

He wanted to hear Kane admit that he lied about smashing his girl in front of everyone.

"Look, I ain't got time for this, dude. I'm here to get my party on. I ain't with this bogus ass shit."

"So now you retracting your muthafuckin' statement, nigga? Is that what this is?" Brandon laughed.

"Look, I don't want no problems, man."

"Of course you don't. I mean, I'mma diplomatic typa nigga so I'm tryna be cool about this shit, you feel me? I ain't wit allat bitchassness you spitting cuz you had a lotta shit to say before, yapping ya gums about how you fucked my bitch."

"It ain't e-even all like what you saying," Kane stuttered.

"Truth be told nigga, I have the urge to smack the fuck outta you right now, but I won't. Cuz you're right, we here to have a good ass time and I don't need no stupid ass assault and battery charges on my shit. But trust me, the next time you even fix your fucking face to say that you can fuck my bitch, I'mma beat the shit outta you, nigga. This pussy right here belongs to me and me only so consider this shit right here some southern hospitality for that ass. I suggest you get your mind right because there will be no more get outta jail free cards."

Kane didn't say a word. He wasn't a punk, but he also wasn't an idiot. He knew that he had gone too far by spreading a silly rumor like that. He just couldn't help but brag about the fact that one of the sexiest girls on campus actually wanted him at some point, and it all just went to his head.

"Aight dude, whatever," Kane muttered.

"Wait a fucking minute!" Legacy screamed.

Legacy had stood back in the corner for a while not saying a word. But after hearing the conversation, she finally understood why Kane had been so distant. He was fucking Mishon and going around school bragging about it. Legacy had suspected that Kane was cheating on her for a while but she never suspected her own best friend would be the trick he was sleeping with.

She was enraged at the thought of Mishon having the upper hand yet again and she snapped.

"You been fucking this bitch and bragging about it, nigga? "

Legacy hit Kane in the chest with her hardest punch. Kane grabbed her by the hand and warned her not to put her hands on him again. He looked over at Tomorrow and wondered how the rumor had turned to him fucking with Mishon when he was really fucking her.

He noticed that Tomorrow seemed unusually calm about the entire situation. In fact, her face read that she was rather amused.

"Hold up. I ain't gonna be too many bitches, ho! I ain't fuckin' ya man!" Mishon yelled.

Mishon's head quickly snapped in Legacy's direction. She was beyond pissed, and at this point, all she needed was a reason to fuck a bitch up. It was bad enough that her man had just created so much drama, but now Legacy wanted to start bugging too? Hell no, she wasn't having it!

"I knew it! Just admit it! You always wanted Kane! You gonna get yours, bitch!" Legacy screamed.

"If you feeling froggy, leap bitch! I ain't wit all this back and forth shit! Act stupid if you want to!" Mishon jumped out of her high-heels.

Tomorrow stood there completely shocked and tickled all at the same time. She had the urge to put her two cents in, but decided against it. She just wanted Kane to grab Legacy and walk away. He looked embarrassed and Tomorrow figured that they should both get out of dodge before they got their asses whipped.

Tomorrow watched as Brandon grabbed Mishon and demanded that she calm down. Mishon knelt down and put her heels back on. She and Brandon were preparing to leave. By the looks of things, Mishon seemed to be calming down, but Tomorrow could tell that Mishon was a little tipsy, and whenever Mishon was tipsy, anything could happen.

Tomorrow walked over to where Brandon stood.

"Aye, take her outta here before she fuck that girl up," she insisted.

"Yeah, we 'bout to roll anyway before we both catch cases in this bitch. Did you ride with her?"

"Yeah, but I'm good. I have a ride. Just make sure y'all call when you hit the hotel."

"I'mma call you," Mishon interrupted. "I'm not that fucked up if that's what you're thinking, but this bitch was about to catch it!" Mishon said putting her arms around Tomorrow. "Okay bitch, I lied. I'm a lil' fucked up."

Both girls laughed.

"Call me when you get situated."

Brandon and Mishon walked to the door, but Mishon wasn't finished telling Legacy off just yet.

"Uh huh, chick, how the fuck you getting home? Looks like somebody's gonna be hittin' the pavement. I suggest you take off those plastic Payless shoes before you do, bitch!"

"That's alright, bitch! You gonna be sangin' a different tune after I tap that ass, just wait!" Legacy yelled.

Brandon walked Mishon to her car. He dug into his

41

pockets and pulled out a bank roll of hundred dollar bills. He removed the rubber band from the roll and counted out a few hundreds.

Mishon got into the car. She picked up her phone and observed a missed call from her mom. She decided to wait and call her back once she got settled in.

"Here, take this." Brandon placed the money in Mishon's hands.

"What's this for?" Mishon asked.

"You said you wanted to get a room tonight, right?"

"Yeah, but ain't you coming?"

"I gotta make a few pit stops first, but I should be there shortly. Where you gon' get the room?"

"How about Hotel Monaco out in Alexandria?"

"Man, you tryna get my ass hemmed the fuck up? I don't fuck with VA like that. The Commonwealth is serious. You better take your fancy ass to the Hyatt downtown and cop a room for tonight and call me once you get it." Brandon walked off.

"Yeah, aight." Mishon sighed.

Mishon turned on the car, blasted her music and sped out of the parking lot. As she drove down the street, she noticed Kane and Legacy standing on the side walk. It looked as if they had been arguing.

She couldn't resist the urge to stop her car. Without warning, she rolled down her windows and started yelling obscenities.

"Bitch now what? What you got to say now?"

Kane stood in front of Legacy to keep her from dashing over to Mishon's car. His blocking her only made her angrier.

"That's okay, bitch, 'cause I'mma see yo' ass in class Monday." Legacy laughed.

42

She angrily stomped her feet behind Kane. She tried her best to escape him but his grip was just too intense.

Mishon parked and exited the car, and slowly walked around to where Legacy stood. Kane grew nervous. He knew that the situation could only get ugly. The girls were friends and he didn't want to see them fighting, especially not in the middle of the street.

He pulled Legacy by the hand and tried to get her to walk away.

"Bitch, I created you!" Mishon yelled as she walked closer. "You wouldn't be shit if it wasn't for me. You would be so fucking irrelevant. Why do you think people know you? Because of me, bitch!"

"You call yourself a friend?" Legacy screamed. "I'mma show you who I really am. Just wait! Fucking my man and smiling all up in my face! I'mma see you for real!"

Kane stood in the middle of the two girls. He didn't want any more altercations going down, at least not tonight. He turned to Legacy in an attempt to stop her from arguing with Mishon.

"Calm the fuck down, Legacy, you know you got asthma. You wanna have a fucking asthma attack out here? I'm not gonna be the one reviving your ass, so pipe the fuck down!" Kane demanded.

Realizing that Kane wasn't going to let her through, Legacy walked off.

Kane turned and stared at Mishon with a guilty look. He knew that he was the cause of all of the drama. Had he kept his lies to himself, no one would be arguing. Besides, he knew that Mishon was out of his league. He had only started the rumor to satisfy his own ego.

"Look Mishon, my bad for what went down. I heard you used to feel a nigga, so I kinda got carried away. I twisted words around, but I ain't mean nothing by it. I hope we can still be cool, but if not, I understand."

"Nah, I ain't got no beef with you. Niggas like you only meet girls like me in your dreams," she replied.

"Wow."

"Look, Brandon done already checked you so we cool. It's your bitch that need to pipe down."

"Just give her some time and all this shit should blow over by Monday." Kane sighed.

"Fuck that! That ho done got away with way too much! And don't act like you don't know. Yeah, I be seein' how she be runnin' over you, nigga. You better put her ass in check! She may be able to punk yo' dumb ass, but not me."

Mishon jumped back into her car and drove off. Kane ran up the street and chased after Legacy. He hoped he'd be able to smooth things over. He was going to need a ride to class on Monday.

"Yo Legacy, wait up!"

"Oh so now you wanna act like you care about me. Nigga, get out of my face with your tired, broke ass. Go catch up with Mishon's ho ass."

"You trying to stay over tonight?"

"For what? You ain't want me there last night. Your punk ass probably had Mishon up in there. No wonder you were pushing me to leave so quick."

"Mishon? Nah baby, it wasn't even like that. I told you that I needed to get some rest for my early class this morning. Plus, my moms told me to chill out on having too much company."

"I looked out for your broke ass! Giving you money, buying you shoes and shit! What you ever do for me? All you gave me was sex, and trust me, it wasn't that great. What have you ever done for me? Shit, maybe I need to start fucking with some real niggas like Brandon!"

Kane got pissed and grabbed Legacy by the arms, forcing her to stand still. Angrily, he pointed his finger directly in her face.

"Look here, I ain't fuck that girl! Some niggas told me she used to feel me and that's all. But don't act like you the best thing that ever happened to me, cuz I can easily fuck with bitches ten times better than you, trust. Your little silly ass think you cute cuz you got that part time gig over at Ruby Tuesdays, but them tips ain't really feeding me, ho!"

Legacy attempted to hold back the tears but it was no use. She caught each tear with her fingertips before they rolled down her cheeks. Kane was unaffected by her tears. To be honest, like everybody else, he was tired of hearing her mouth.

"How the fuck are you going to tell me I ain't do nothing for you?" Kane yelled. "Bitch, how many times yo' mother told you to find somewhere else to spend the night cuz she wanted her man to stay over? And your ungrateful ass came straight to my house! Now, I get why people don't fuck with yo ass."

"And why is that?" Legacy cried.

"Because you act all stuck up, but ain't got shit. You driving a nineteen eighty whatever the fuck that is, you stay in a one-bedroom shoe box apartment, and then you wanna act snotty?" Kane laughed.

He was so done with playing games with Legacy. It's true he had cheated on her, but she didn't make it any easier on him. He tried to be a good boyfriend in the beginning but her constant nagging and overbearing ways just pushed him further and further away.

Kane didn't understand why Legacy couldn't just be more like Tomorrow or Mishon. They were both laid back females who enjoyed a good time. They weren't trying to act like they were better than anyone, they just had that natural swag about them. Legacy just didn't get the memo.

Kane was tired of trying to make Legacy into someone he knew she would never become.

"Go find a nigga like Brandon and see if he will tolerate your stupid ass, cuz I'm done. Hmph, what am I saying? You ain't even got the right mind frame to deal with a nigga like that." He laughed.

Kane finally let go of Legacy's arms and walked away. He left her there alone in the middle of the street. Legacy had no idea where she was because she didn't frequent D.C., especially not the south-side. Scared to death, she decided to call her mom.

"Hello, Mom?"

"Yeah."

"Do you think that you can pick me up? I'm kind of stranded."

"Where's your car, Legacy?" her mom asked in an annoyed tone.

"It's parked outside our apartment."

"Well how did you get over there?"

"I rode with Mishon and Tomorrow, but Mishon left the party early. Look, can you just please pick me up?"

"Goddamnit, Legacy!" her mom screamed into the phone. "It's bad enough that since you were born, I've had to work all damn day and night cuz your father never paid child support. You're grown and I'm still taking care of your ass. Grow the fuck up, Legacy!"

"Just come get me, Ma!" Legacy screamed back.

"Just when I get a little me time, you call with this shit? I was hoping that you would spend the night over a friend's house tonight. Take your ass back to the party and call me when you get there! Shit!"

Legacy's mom hung up on her. She did as her mother told her and walked back to Trell's house. Once there, she sat on the curb in front of his house and called her mom to give her directions. After being cursed out for the second time, she sat on the curb looking pitiful and slowly devised a plan to get back at the people who had just humiliated her.

"Kane and Mishon definitely gon' see who I really am, just watch!"

CHAPTER

~ 4 ~

ishon caught the elevator up to the eighteenth floor of the hotel. She had finally made it to the room and all she wanted to do was relax. When she opened the door, she gasped at how beautiful and spacious the room was.

I guess the Hyatt was a good choice after all, she thought.

She had purchased a one-bedroom suite with a full kitchen and everything was laid out. Mishon was happy that she could enjoy a night of peace and quiet without the bothersome sounds of her mom's boyfriend.

She sent Brandon a text letting him know where the spot was.

"Ugh!" She moaned while throwing her bag on the bed.

"My feet are killing me."

After kicking off her Jimmy Choo platforms, she prepared a hot bubble bath in the room's oversized bath tub.

Oh shit, let me send Tomorrow a text to see if she's okay Mishon remembered.

She scrolled down to Tomorrow's name and decided to call instead, but she only caught her voicemail.

"Hey, it's me, Shon. Just wondering if you made it home safe. Call me when you get this message cuz I got some shit to tell you. Bye, bitch." She said playfully before hanging up.

Mishon finally undressed and walked into the bathroom. As soon as she stepped into the water, she heard a knock at the door.

She grabbed a guest bath robe off the back of the bathroom door and slid it on.

"There goes my baby."

She anxiously ran to the door but when she looked through the peephole, she didn't see anyone there.

"What the fuck?"

She cracked the door slightly, just enough to peek through the crack, and saw flowers lying in front of the door.

"Ooh, my favorite." Mishon admired the flowers as she bent down and picked them up.

"So I take it you like them?" She heard a sexy voice ask.

Mishon knew who was standing over her. She sniffed the pink roses and smirked.

"So I guess you want some tonight, huh?"

"If you don't mind."

She stood up and gave Brandon a tight hug and a long French kiss.

"I drew us a hot bubble bath," Mishon seductively spoke.

Brandon took her by the hand and allowed her to guide

him into the room.

"That sounds good, cuz a nigga can really use one right about now. I had a stressful night." He laughed.

Mishon sat on the bed and helped Brandon undress. She admired his swag. Brandon always stayed fresh from his button ups, down to his retro Jordans. He kept a clean shape up with shiny, huge rocks hanging out of each ear. It was only right for Mishon to be his girl.

Brandon walked naked over to the closet and hung up his clothes. He knew that Mishon was watching him and he wanted to remind her of exactly what she had.

"You roll up yet?" Brandon smiled.

"I got a half of blunt we can finish."

Brandon dipped his 6'3" sculpted, caramel body into the bath first and Mishon quickly followed. She nestled herself between his legs. They sparked a blunt which in return sparked a conversation about the party they had just left.

"Can you believe that bitch had the nerve to disrespect me like that?" Mishon said in an aggravated tone.

"Don't worry about it, she fucking with a bum nigga. I seen him in the hallways a few times, but I ain't never really talk to the nigga. I know y'all ain't fuck, but ain't nobody gonna straight disrespect me and mines."

"Yeah, I see what you sayin'."

"Don't even trip off these bust downs. Legacy ain't got shit on you. It looks like she trying to be like you and your girl Tomorrow anyway. But watch your back with Legacy, cuz you know she be starting shit."

"I hear that, but she don't want it with me for real."

After their bath, Mishon and Brandon settled into bed and decided to watch a little TV before they dozed off. Mishon searched the channels until she made her way to FOX 5 News.

She knew that they'd be doing a story on the Lipstick

Serial Killer and she wanted to hear all of the details. She had become slightly obsessed with the Kiss of Death and couldn't explain why. It was almost as if she had an unspoken connection with this woman although she had never even laid eyes on her.

Mishon waited patiently until she heard the story that she was waiting for.

"Baby, do we have to watch this shit?" Brandon asked in a disturbed tone.

"Shhh. Nigga this shit is better than prime time TV. Shit like this don't just happen everyday. We got a killer on the loose!" Mishon anxiously replied.

"You getting obsessed with this shit."

"Shhh. Listen, listen!"

"Back to our biggest story of the night," the reporter began. "The Lipstick Serial Killer that we like to call the 'Kiss of Death' seems to be maintaining quite a low profile. There hasn't been a murder in over a week, but we are sure that she will strike again. The question is why is she doing this? Is she just a cold-blooded psycho killer, or could she simply be a woman scorned? We have interviewed professional psychologists who suggest that this is definitely a possibility."

"Nah, that bitch just crazy as shit!" Mishon yelled at the TV.

She grabbed the remote to turn up the volume and sat up in bed. Brandon shook his head as he watched how consumed Mishon had become.

The news reporter continued to discuss the Lipstick Serial Killer in detail. Mishon watched patiently, but she wouldn't say a word.

"Here are the facts: we know that the Lipstick Serial Killer is very detailed and distinct in her killing. In every murder, she uses two main

accessories: a butcher knife and designer lipstick.

After testing the lipstick print on several of the victims' foreheads, we now know that the Kiss of Death is using Tom Ford's Scarlet Rouge Lipstick. We suspect that whoever she is, she is a woman of expensive taste and prides herself in precision."

Mishon's eyes grew wide. She stared at the screen like she had just seen a ghost. Brandon looked at Mishon with a confused stare. He didn't understand why she was in such shock by what she had heard.

"What the hell is wrong with you?" Brandon laughed.

"You ain't hear that? They said that bitch uses Scarlet Rouge Lipstick. I only know two people who wear that shit: me and Tomorrow."

Brandon burst into laughter. He couldn't believe what he was hearing.

"So what you think Tomorrow is a killa?" Brandon teased.

"Nigga, shut up."

"Or maybe y'all on some Laverne and Shirley type shit, huh?"

"Nigga, Laverne and Shirley? Those are the chicks from Nick at Nite, you mean Thelma and Louise."

"Yeah, them bitches too. Baby listen, you are too obsessed with this shit. That lipstick shit is just a coincidence. Y'all like the finer things in life, so it only makes sense that y'all would have some shit like that. It's lipstick. Anybody could have some of that shit."

"I can't help it. It's just so addicting. But, yeah, you're right." Mishon sighed.

"Besides, you and Tomorrow are both too damn bougie to be killing anybody. If blood even got anywhere near y'all eight hundred dollar Manolos, you two would fuckin' lose it!" Brandon laughed.

"I'm not bougie. I just have sophisticated taste."

"Suuuure. Anyway, you just gotta stop it with all this killer shit. You starting to make a nigga nervous."

"Oh, I got you nervous baby? Don't worry, I won't kill you just yet. I'mma at least wait 'til I got that ring on my finger," Mishon joked.

"Aight, don't get fucked up, Shon."

Mishon giggled. She leaned over and placed a kiss on Brandon's forehead.

"Aye, you better cut that shit out!" Brandon yelled.

Mishon sat and watched the remainder of the report. She knew that she was a little too obsessed with the Lipstick Serial Killer, but it was exciting to watch and get updates. There hadn't been a serial killer in the DMV since the D.C. Sniper, and everyone wanted to know where the Kiss of Death would strike next, especially Mishon.

CHAPTER

~ 5 ~

his shit aint over bitch!

"My sentiments exactly."

Tomorrow laughed to herself before erasing the text message.

She walked into her bedroom and rested on her queen size bed. She was finally glad to be home and after a rough weekend, all she wanted to do was sleep. She heard footsteps clicking down the hallway and she knew that her rest would be short lived.

Tomorrow's mom peeked her head inside the door.

"Oh, you're finally home. You didn't show up to church yesterday. Where were you?" Her mother questioned.

"Just hanging out for the weekend."

"What's wrong with you? You seem a little off. Did you take your meds today? Tomorrow you know you have to keep up with that medicine, it's nothing to play around with. Now I know you're young and you want to have your fun, but you have to be more respon—"

"Mom, I know!" Tomorrow interrupted. "I'm just stressing okay, with school and everything. Ugh, I took the medicine. Please just leave me alone."

"Well, I have some good news." Tomorrow's mom changed the subject.

"What is it?"

"Well, Deacon Bell's son Micah is home from school, and I told him all the good things you're doing with your music and writing. You know he's studying to be a pastor. Such a responsible and respectful young man, and I just thought that he'd be good for you."

"No."

"No? What do you mean no. Young respectable men don't come around every day."

"I said no, Mom."

"Well, it's too late. The deacon and I already set it up, and I hear he's really excited about taking you out."

"How are you gonna set me up on a date without my permission?"

Tomorrow was angry. Her mother always did things like that and she couldn't stand it.

Janet held Tomorrow to a very high standard. She was only a high school graduate, but managed to build a very lucrative career in Chicago as an interior decorator for some very prominent people. When they moved from Chicago to D.C. nearly ten years ago, Janet pushed even harder to make a name for herself. Everything was about the image.

56

Although she never really explained her reasoning, she demanded nothing but the best from her daughter. The truth was; Janet always knew that there was something a little different about Tomorrow but she refused to acknowledge it. Her way of dealing with Tomorrow's internal struggles was to simply force her to be great.

So naturally, Tomorrow adopted that same mentality; always striving for perfection or at least playing the part. Unfortunately, that her search for perfection secretly killed her on the inside.

She had to be the best. The best student, the best daughter, the best Christian. Tomorrow struggled with an internal tug of war that consumed her and she just couldn't seem to escape it.

"You're going. I give you all the freedom in the world. You could at least do this one thing for your mother."

"Freedom? Wellsa massa, I'ze eighteen now and Iza free from your wrath. Oh happy day!"

"Tomorrow!" Janet screeched.

"Ughh. Fine. When is the damn date?" Tomorrow slipped.

"I know you better watch your mouth in my house. Are you crazy?" Janet scolded.

"I just said I had a long weekend. I just need...when is the date, Ma?"

"Next Friday. I gave him your number, so he'll be calling you with the details."

"Okay."

"Don't mess this up. Make sure you go get your locs retwisted before the date. Your edges looking kinda nappy, and we don't want him thinking you gonna be giving him some nappy headed babies." Janet laughed.

I oughta sock the fuck outta this bitch for that comment,

Tomorrow thought. "Okay."

"And don't forget to take that chipped nail polish off your toes. It looks kinda tacky and you know better than that. As a matter of fact, how much is in your account?"

"Three thousand, three hundred dollars."

"Good. I'm going to set up an appointment down at the spa. Get the works."

"Okay, Mom."

Tomorrow was getting angrier by the second. Why couldn't her mom do this another time? All she wanted to do was rest before she kirked the fuck out.

"Most importantly, remember. It's about—"

"I know, Mom, it's about the image," Tomorrow said dryly.

"Exactly. Don't make me look bad. If things go well, you'll have you a nice, fine pastor-to-be for a husband and I'll have a respectable son-in-law who adds to the brand. Don't mess it up."

"Goodbye, Ma."

Janet kissed her daughter on the forehead and smiled before walking out.

"Get some rest," Janet said as she peeped her head back in the door.

"I was trying to, bitch," Tomorrow whispered under her breath.

***

Tomorrow dreaded getting up the next morning. She hadn't slept very well the night before, and after hitting the snooze button on her alarm clock six times, she realized that it wouldn't stop buzzing until she got up. Her body ached and she felt like she had to vomit.

"What the fuck is wrong with me?"

Tomorrow rushed to her bathroom and threw up in the

toilet. She wiped the excess with her hand towel and opened her medicine cabinet. She searched the cabinet for her pills and popped three small tablets. When she closed the cabinet, she noticed her reflection staring back at her.

Flashbacks of the weekend held her attention for a few moments. Rage filled her heart and revenge bellowed in the pit of her belly. She knew what she had to do.

Before stepping into the shower, she took one more look into the mirror and gave a wicked grin. She puckered up and kissed her reflection.

Once she arrived at school, she knew she had to find Mishon. She hadn't talked to her all weekend and she had a lot that she had to get off her chest.

When she walked into the building, she immediately headed towards Mishon's first class and waited for her. A few moments later, Mishon appeared.

"Bitch, where the fuck you been at? I aint heard from your ass since Friday," Mishon yelled.

"Girl, it's a long story. I got some shit to tell yo' ass."

"I called you. Chick, you won't believe what the fuck happened after the party. And, oh my gosh, guess what?"

"What?"

"You know that dude Quan you was dancing with at the party?"

"Uh huh." Tomorrow remembered exactly who he was.

"Well, he got fucked up over the weekend. Like hospitalized type shit. He know who did it, but he ain't saying shit. And I ain't sure if this part is true, but I heard that someone fucked his car up!" Mishon laughed.

"On that shit, somebody wrote: *Eat this since you like stealing pussy...* Aaaaand they had like six dead cats spread the fuck out on this nigga sun roof!" Mishon squealed.

"Bitch, shut up, you lying!" Tomorrow laughed.

"I'm so serious. He done fucked with the wrong one, I guess. That bitch gotta be something serious if she killing cats over this nigga."

"That's crazy as hell. See that's what happen when you mess with these bum ass bitches. Damn man, that's crazy! Ooh, I needed that laugh." Tomorrow laughed even harder.

"Why must I feel like that, why must I chase the cat?!" Tomorrow sang.

The two girls burst into uncontrollable laughter. They couldn't believe that something like that had happened, especially in Quan's hood. That kind of thing only happened in the movies.

"Wow. I really can't believe it," Tomorrow said wiping the tears from her eyes.

"Yeah, shit just got real." Mishon giggled. "But anyway, what you have to tell me?"

"We gotta talk like after school."

"Oh damn, that deep, huh?" Mishon giggled.

"You know it. Anyway, I have Bible study tonight, so just meet up at my spot at like 8:30."

"Aight. Well, I'll see you in Intro to Logic."

"Wait, speaking of our Logic class... Have you talked to Legacy?"

"Hell nah. Fuck that ho!" Mishon exclaimed. "How about as I was leaving the party, I had an encounter with that ass. She threatened me and everything, but she didn't have much to say yesterday. She heated now though, cuz Kane don't want shit to do with her anymore. She been running around here following his ass and he won't say a word."

"Damn. I knew that shit wouldn't last anyway." Tomorrow giggled.

"Y'all still gettin' it in?" Mishon questioned.

"We did last week, but that bitch came over and fucked

up the groove. I think it's a wrap with that situation. I mean, he has great dick, but he's a lame. Plus, now he done been chumped by Brandon. Not a good look at all! Trust me, it's a wrap. Like Reynolds."

"Oh word?"

"Yeah, girl. He's like last week's news. I may test it once more, though," Tomorrow joked.

"Well, I just wish this bitch would get the fuck off my back, cuz I don't want her dude."

"Don't knock it 'til you try it," Tomorrow teased.

"Nah, I'm good."

"Girl, let me get my ass to class before I'm late. Don't forget to come to my house tonight."

"Aight, later."

Mishon raced to make it to class on time. She passed Brandon in the hallway rapping to his boys, but had no time to fuck around. Maintaining her 3.2 grade point average meant everything to her. She had to be the complete package, beauty and brains.

As she entered her Intro to Journalism class, she noticed that Professor Lawrence was already beginning his lesson, and he hated being interrupted by latecomers.

"Oh, there you are Mishon."

Mishon sat down and pulled out her study materials. She already knew that he would put her on blast. She had been the target of his wrath on many occasions.

"And why are we late this time, young lady?" Professor Lawrence inquired.

"Be for real, I was only like two seconds late."

Immediately, there was tension. Professor Lawrence couldn't stand students like Mishon: students who had horrible attitudes, but were basically untouchable because of their good grades.

Mishon had a quick temper and she didn't have any objections to giving you a piece of her mind. Anything was liable to set her off.

Her classmates stared at her as they sat in complete silence wondering what would happen next.

"Young lady, you're late because your behind wasn't in that chair when class began."

"So what you gonna do about that?"

The entire class snickered and whispered to one another.

"Get the hell out of my class!" Professor Lawrence screamed as he pointed to the door.

Mishon was pissed. She hated being put on blast, but she knew it was her own fault. Luckily, she had already taken midterms, so she knew she wouldn't be missing much. She grabbed her belongings and prepared to exit the classroom.

When Mishon approached the professor's desk, she stopped and stared coldly at him. Before exiting, she dug inside her backpack, pulled out her homework, and tossed her paper onto his lap.

"Here's my homework. Peace, bitches!" she sassed while switching out the door.

What am I going to do now? she pondered as she walked through the empty hallway. Got another forty-five minutes to kill."

She noticed Legacy randomly walking up the hallway snacking uncontrollably on a bag of chips.

Tsk, here come this trick, Mishon thought.

As Legacy got closer, she grew excited to see Mishon. Almost as if nothing had ever happened. She rushed towards her with a shocked expression.

"Oh, it's just you," she muttered.

"Yeah, it's me bitch, in the flesh," Mishon snapped.

She dropped her book bag to the floor and prepared for war. She thought Legacy had come to fight and she was all but ready to lay hands on her.

"Girl, please, don't nobody want to fight you. Besides, I don't feel too well this morning and I would hate to throw up all over your pretty new weave."

"What the fuck are you talking about? See, I knew your ass was crazy!" Mishon exclaimed.

Legacy laughed hysterically and continued to walk by.

That ho got something up her sleeve. She ain't fooling nobody.

The next class Mishon had was Intro to Logic, along with Tomorrow, Kane and Legacy.

This time, she refused to be late. She walked in the classroom and found Kane sitting in the front of the class. Legacy was peering at him from the back of the room like a homicidal maniac.

"Is this seat taken?" Mishon asked loudly, hoping to capture Legacy's attention.

"Nah, you can sit there if you want. Here, let me pull out your chair," Kane volunteered.

"Why, thank you."

Mishon sat down and peered at Legacy from the corner of her eye. She whipped out her Mac red lip gloss and started applying it to her thick pink lips. Kane couldn't help but to stare.

"So is everything cool?" He questioned with a soft tone.

"Why wouldn't it be?"

Kane peeked over his shoulder to make sure Legacy wasn't listening in on what he was about to say.

"Why didn't you tell me that you liked me a long time ago?"

"You started dating Legacy and I ain't a hater, so I just let it go. But I'm glad it worked out this way because had I not moved on, I would've never met Brandon, and he is too good to lose."

"I ain't mean no disrespect, but you're sexy as hell, so I got all caught up and thought that maybe we could—you know?"

"Uh, no. Consider this a warning and watch your mouth 'cause I ain't that chick."

"I can respect that. I always did like that about you, you know? Your style."

Mishon rolled her eyes.

Tomorrow walked in one minute before the class began. She peeped the scene between Mishon and Kane and figured that Mishon was up to no good.

"Hey, Legacy," Tomorrow greeted Legacy before sitting behind Mishon.

"Umm hmm," Legacy replied as she stared dead at Kane.

Dr. Kremp finally walked into the classroom with her suitcase and prepared to begin her lecture.

"Okay, ladies and gentlemen. Pull out your books and flip to page 216. In our last meeting, we discussed the modern philosophy of Rene Descartes.

She turned on the overhead projector and displayed some of the chapter's vocabulary words.

"Can anyone tell me one of the first philosophies we discussed last week?"

Tomorrow raised her hand.

"Yes, Tomorrow?"

"We discussed the absolutism involved with certainty. The foundation of knowledge is certainty. We can doubt our senses and our inferences, but certainty is what is impossible to doubt. It is important to check all beliefs by first examining their foundations."

"Correct. Very good. Sounds like someone has actually

been reading," the teacher praised Tomorrow.

Tomorrow was the top student in the class and made no apologies about how intelligent she was. Once she received her degree, she planned to do several case studies on the correlation between nymphomaniacs and mental illness so that she could finish writing her first book.

Tomorrow had big plans for her book. She used both real people and real life situations to make sure that her book was perfect. With her keen ability to tap into the resources around her, her book would be a nice blend between a standard nonfiction book of psychological studies and the warped reality of a romance novel gone awry.

This was something that had never been done. Once her book was released, she had no doubt that it would change the world of psychology and literary fiction forever.

Tomorrow had to be the best, and sometimes being the best meant that you had to do things unconventionally in order to succeed. She had definitely done that and had no doubt in her mind that ultimately things would work out just as she planned.

Thanks to her mother's consistent push towards perfection, not only was Tomorrow going to be a successful author, but she was musically gifted as well. She vowed to be the best at everything she touched. Intelligent, talented, and hardworking, from the outside it appeared as if she had it all together. But of course, most of it was a facade.

She was admired by many, but not everyone was fond of Tomorrow's perfection. Legacy was definitely one of those people who weren't pleased with her.

She hated the fact that in everyone's eyes, Tomorrow could do no wrong, especially to Mishon.

Legacy couldn't stand the fact that Tomorrow had just shown up from Chicago one day and stole her best friend right up from under her nose. She had come in and flashed her money along with a witty smile and like magic, Legacy's best friend was gone. Because of that, Legacy secretly hated Tomorrow and was always searching for that one thing that would prove Tomorrow's good image was nothing but a fake. Her plan was to eventually turn Mishon against her. Unfortunately, Legacy could never find anything worthy enough to tarnish her image. Tomorrow appeared to be squeaky clean, but that didn't stop Legacy from hating.

Legacy smacked her teeth at the teacher's praise of Tomorrow. When everyone looked in her direction, she began snacking loudly on her bag of chips.

"Excuse me, but you're being a bit rude," Mishon pointed out.

"Well, if it wasn't for Kane, I wouldn't be eating like this," Legacy stated while licking chip residue off her fingers.

Kane looked back at Legacy and mugged her. He wondered what the fuck she was talking about. Dr. Kremp turned around and stared at Legacy.

"Excuse me. I'm sure you read the syllabus, and it clearly states that no food is allowed in this room."

"But the doctor said that I have to eat periodically so I won't throw up. This is the only way I can keep the food down," Legacy whined.

"Well, unless you have a doctor's note, I'm going to have to ask you to put the chips away. Class will be over soon, and I'm sure you can wait."

Legacy rolled her eyes.

I bet if Tomorrow was eating chips, you wouldn't give two fucks, she thought to herself.

"If you feel sick to your stomach, then quickly excuse yourself and go to the nearest bathroom. Understood?"

"I guess."

The whole class kept a close eye on Legacy waiting for her to do something else dramatic. Legacy watched as Mishon and Tomorrow whispered to one another.

"You hear that?" Mishon asked.

"What?" Tomorrow replied.

"All that talk about the doctor and having to eat. Don't you get it? She's pregnant!"

Kane couldn't help overhearing their conversation.

Pregnant? I know that bitch ain't pregnant by me, he thought.

In another attempt to get attention, Legacy began gasping for air. Her nonsense disturbed the lesson once again and Dr. Kremp was definitely not happy about it. Legacy rocked back and forth and placed her hand over her mouth.

Everybody knew she was putting on a show, even Dr. Kremp.

"Enough, Legacy." Dr. Kremp stopped the lesson.

"I'm not going to tolerate these disruptions in my class. What are you trying to prove?"

Legacy continued to play sick. She hoped that everyone would eventually get the hint.

Both Kane and Mishon gave her the evil eye.

"Can I please talk to Kane in the hallway, Dr. Kremp?"

"Legacy, this is an hour and fifteen minute class. You've already wasted thirty of those minutes with your nonsense. Now you will have ample time to talk to him on your own time. Don't interrupt my class again!"

"That bitch fakin', Dr. Kremp," Mishon blurted out.

"Shut your ass up before I get up out this chair!" Legacy threatened.

"You sitting there fake acting like you pregnant and shit. But probably got a tampon in right now."

"Why are you so fucking concerned about my pregnancy? This shit is between me and Kane. You wack ass bitch!"

"You and your funky ass mama," Mishon snapped.

Dr. Kremp had heard enough. She turned off the projector and looked over at Legacy and Mishon.

"Enough. I want the both of you to shut your mouths or get the hell outta here!"

An eerie silence took over the classroom. The girls sat back in their seats and didn't utter another word.

Tomorrow looked over at Kane and noticed his embarrassment. She could see the anger slowly brewing within him and could tell that he was about to explode. She swiftly packed up her things and looked over at Mishon, hoping she would do the same.

"Girl, come on," Tomorrow suggested.

"For what?"

"Girl, look at Kane's face!"

Mishon looked at Kane. He looked like he was ready to kirk off and they all knew he was capable of flipping shit over. He was 6'4" and 250 pounds of pure destruction.

Tomorrow tugged on Mishon's arm.

"Come on, bitch," she demanded.

Before either of them could move, Legacy stirred things back up.

"Kane, I need to talk to you about our baby!"

"Listen bitch, you ain't pregnant with my kid! I strap up every time with yo' ass. Sit the fuck down and shut up." Kane's light tone quickly turned red.

"That's it. All of you out! And you better believe I'm going to have a talk with the Dean about this!"

Dr. Kremp looked over at Legacy, Kane and Mishon. She pointed to the door with a look of disgust.

Fearing that more trouble would erupt, Kane and Mishon quickly gathered their things and exited the classroom.

After a few moments, Legacy emerged.

"Fuck you, nigga. You gon' take care of your responsibilities. You a no good nigga. How you gon' fuck me then act like you ain't the daddy?" Legacy yelled as she entered the hallway.

"Stay the fuck back there! I swear to God bitch, I will fuck your life up if you get any closer," Kane warned.

Legacy inched towards Kane. She wanted to make a scene. She lived for the times when people stopped and actually paid attention to her, but she didn't understand that not all attention was necessarily good attention.

"I fucking hate you!" Kane yelled.

Mishon stood back because she wasn't sure of what Kane would do next, but she didn't want to leave just yet. This argument was getting good.

"Good, nigga I hate you too, and I wish you would try and hit me," Legacy said.

Kane cocked his arm back but quickly put it down. He didn't want to hit Legacy, but his adrenaline was at an all time high. He knew he had to get out before he did something he was going to regret. He walked closer to the exit door.

"Yeah, go ahead. Leave, you punk ass nigga!" Legacy taunted.

"I can't stand you, bitch!"

Tomorrow slipped out of the classroom to find Mishon. She wanted to make sure that everything was good, but once she entered the hallway, she realized that she was caught in the middle of yet another dramatic scene.

She watched as Legacy chuckled at the commotion she had caused. No longer was she grabbing her stomach. Her "morning sickness" had magically disappeared.

This bitch is getting outta control. Tomorrow shook her head and walked over to Mishon.

"You just don't listen do you? I said let's go, bitch," Tomorrow insisted as she pulled Mishon towards the parking lot.

"Wait, it was getting good!" Mishon whispered.

"Nigga, you a pussy ass nigga and I can't wait to take your ass for child support!" Legacy screamed.

Kane didn't respond. He walked through the exit door and headed for the bus stop, but Legacy wouldn't give up that easily.

She followed him. Her car was parked not too far from the bus bay, so she decided to have a little fun.

"Yeah, nigga, keep walking. You ain't shit and your dick ain't shit either. Wit' yo' broke ass, spending up my money and shit. Keep fucking walking!" Legacy laughed.

Kane stopped in his tracks. He was tired of Legacy's childish ways. He saw Legacy's car, and without thinking, ran over to it and aggressively kicked her windshield with all of his force.

Everyone stood in awe of what had just happened. Legacy's eyes grew wide with fear and she stood there unable to speak.

"I told you to stop fucking with me, bitch! Now drive home in your broke up shit!"

Kane limped towards the bus stop. It was apparent that he had hurt himself from that power kick. He was bleeding through his jeans, and yet, he seemed almost unaffected.

Seeing Kane kick in that windshield was all that Mishon and Tomorrow needed to see. It was time to go. They simply refused to be witnesses to anything.

After experiencing all the drama, Tomorrow and Mishon decided to take the rest of the day off. They maintained pretty good GPAs and knew it would be no big deal to miss a few classes.

"Bitch, can you believe that shit?" Mishon asked as she entered Tomorrow's car.

"I told you to bring your punk ass on. I know when a muthafucka is about to snap the fuck off. You wanted to sit there and enjoy the show and shit. That nigga coulda pulled a Columbine out here. No thank you!" Tomorrow laughed.

"Steam was rising out that nigga scalp. I ain't know what the fuck to do!" Mishon laughed too.

"That nigga crazy as hell. But I think that shit kinda just turned me the fuck on. I think I'mma call his ass tonight. He needs to give my pussy a goodbye kiss."

"Not with that broke ass leg, he won't. He gon' need stitches, boo, no dick for you."

"I know right. Nigga think he Jackie Chan and shit."

"Girl, you stupid as hell. Stop here. There's my car over there. So what we doing?" Mishon asked changing the subject.

"Let's go to the spa. My treat. My mom is on some crazy shit right now, but I'll tell you 'bout it later. Follow me."

"Aight bet."

CHAPTER

~ 6 ~

*M*ishon exited Tomorrow's car and got into her own. She was excited about going to the spa. That was really the only place that the two girls could talk freely and candidly about life.

They had fun getting facials and pedicures too, but most of all, it was really just their time to release.

Once they arrived at Mona's Spa and Wellness Center, they prepared to be pampered like true princesses. The spa was located in Reston, Virginia, far enough away from the center of the DMVto feel like they were on a getaway vacation.

"Welcome back to Mona's Spa and Wellness Center, ladies. What can we do for you today?" Mona asked.

"Everything. We need the works, Mo," Tomorrow responded.

"Okay, great. I'll start you girls off with a full body massage. You two will be in room 8 with Stephanie and April. They are the best massage therapists here. There are fresh robes and towels in the rooms, so strip down in there, and they will be with you shortly."

"Thanks so much," Tomorrow replied.

The girls walked into the room and put down their bags. They found the closet that held the fresh robes and each of them grabbed one.

Both girls stripped down to their panties and slipped on their robes. Mishon noticed a huge bruise under Tomorrow's ribs. Tomorrow tried to ignore the fact that Mishon was staring at her but she knew that she would eventually have to explain.

"Yeah, trick, I seen it. What the fuck happened to you?" Mishon questioned.

"I got into a fight."

"With who?"

"This dude. Don't worry, I won."

"Bitch, you sure?" Mishon laughed.

"Shut up, ho. I don't wanna talk about it. Just know that nigga is old news now," Tomorrow assured.

"I hope so, cuz we too fly to be on that Ike and Tina shit."

The girls laid down on the parallel massage tables and waited for their masseuses. Once Stephanie and April began the session, the girls relaxed. Mona was right, these two were definitely the best massage therapists the girls had ever had.

"So…" Mishon began. What did you have to tell me that you couldn't tell me at school?"

Tomorrow thought about telling Mishon the truth. But honestly, she just wasn't ready to deal with it just yet. So she decided to bring up her mother setting her up on a date.

"Well, how about my mother and a deacon at my church set me up with the deacon's son."

"What you mean set you up?"

"These niggas told him that I would go out on a date with him. I feel like a fucking mail order bride or some shit. My mom's all like Oh he's a good catch and he'll add to the brand. All she cares about is her damn image. If she knew what was really going on, she'd have a fucking heart attack. How the hell are you gonna set somebody up on a date without them knowing?" Tomorrow complained.

"I feel you. That shit is fucked up, but you never know, T. You may actually like him." Mishon giggled.

"Bitch, he the son of a deacon, he's studying to be a pastor, and I know he ain't slanging no dick. So why in the hell am I talking to him again?" Tomorrow laughed.

"It's only one date. I'm pretty sure they ain't gonna force this nigga on you. Besides, one sniff of your jezebel ass and he's gonna go running for the hills anyway."

"Fuck you, ho. And you obviously don't know my mom. She will make sure that I don't fuck up her dream. She's been trying to get me and Micah together since we came to VA. She's basically already planning the wedding."

"Well, cheers to you, bitch," Mishon joked.

"We can make Legacy's baby the flower girl," Tomorrow said.

"Good luck with that chick. Last time I checked, fake fetuses don't frequent arranged marriages."

"I can't stand you." Tomorrow laughed uncontrollably. "But enough about me–how's the home life?"

"Bitch, that shit is non fucking existent. I've been basically staying with Brandon. Between his house and these jazzy ass hotels, I haven't really seen my mom or that wack ass nigga in days," Mishon explained. "We had a run in a few days ago when I was on the way to your house. He gon' try and stop me from leaving out the house. This negro had the nerve to tell me that I couldn't go nowhere until I respected him as the man of the house!"

"Word?" Tomorrow didn't say too much.

"Yes, girl. Man of the fucking house! Are you fucking kidding me? Nigga, how you the man of the house and you don't pay not one mutherfuckin' bill? Not one. He think his pretty ass can just flash a smile and all is good, but fuck that. My mom need to kick that ass to the curb."

"That's crazy."

"I know, and with my mom working all these crazy ass hours at the airport, who knows what the fuck this nigga is up to. He got the entire house to himself all fucking day. I already know that nigga on some foul ass shit. But whatever, if my mom thinks this bum ass nigga is her happily ever after, so be it!"

It was apparent that Mishon had an utter distaste for her mom's boyfriend. Part of her hatred for him stemmed from the fact that she never really had her mother. For most of her life, her mother was either too involved in her work or a man to even really be concerned about what Mishon was doing. She hated the fact that her mother didn't understand that although jobs and men may come and go, Mishon was going to be her daughter forever.

Mishon once longed for a true mother/daughter relationship, but eventually gave up hope when her mom's live-in dude came around. If she could be put on the back burner for a man who couldn't even help take care of the household, Mishon knew that there was no way she would ever have a true relationship with her mother. She swore to herself that she'd never sell out like her mother did. She was not only going to make sure she had a good looking man, he was going to be both a protector and a provider.

Those were the same qualities that made her fall for Brandon. He always had her back no matter what and she loved that about him. The fact that he was her idea of what a perfect man should be, even at such a young age, let her know that she had done well for herself.

She didn't get how a forty-something year old man still didn't have his life together when a twenty-year-old seemed to have it all figured out.

"Well, I'm just glad you got your mind right. Cuz we ain't on no bum ass niggas," Tomorrow stated.

"No doubt, my baby Brandon holds me down and I ain't never letting that nigga go. Maybe somebody will come end this nigga so that my mom can get her mind right too," Mishon added.

"Yeah," Tomorrow replied. "Maybe they will."

CHAPTER

~ 7 ~

his just in: the Kiss of Death has struck again, this time in Arlington, Virginia, a mere twenty-two miles from the last murder. Thirty-five year old Craig Johnson was found in his Arlington apartment, bound with multiple stab wounds to his chest and a lipstick print on his forehead. He was found by a close relative who quickly called 911 when he discovered Johnson. There is no word as to whether or not there were any witnesses, but if anyone has any information on this crime or the Lipstick Serial Killer, please call the number at the bottom of the screen."

Marcus watched intensely as the reporter announced yet another Lipstick murder in the DMV area. There had already been a total of five murders within the last two months and it had everyone on edge. Everyone wondered when the

Kiss of Death would strike next.

Her victims were all African American men between the ages of 21 and 40, from all different walks of life. They all had two things in common: they were all very attractive and living on their own. Every scene was set up similarly in what looked to be an extremely intense sex escapade that went awry. Most importantly, all of her murders were sealed with a venomous kiss to the forehead.

"Turn the TV off and come drink of some of this," Tomorrow said.

"Damn, you do me so good. Where have you been all my life?"

Tomorrow walked from the kitchen and handed Marcus a lovely mixture of Ciroc, Pineapple and a splash of Sprite. She sat down next to him on the couch and snatched the remote.

"There, that's better," she said after turning off the television.

"You know what would be even better?" Marcus said while sipping his drink.

"What is that?" Tomorrow asked seductively.

"You on top of me."

"I'm sure we could arrange that."

Marcus got up from the couch and led Tomorrow into his bedroom. They had only known each other for a few days, but Marcus was enamored by Tomorrow's personality. Not only was she beautiful, she was articulate, witty and so easy to talk to. But what he liked about her the most was her sensuality. She made him want her without being overtly forward. There was just something about her, and he would finally get the chance to experience her in rare form.

Marcus pulled his wife beater over his soft, butterscotch skin. He revealed a body that had a few extra pounds to love.

On his chest was a tattoo of the head of a half man and half lion and a pencil shaped scar that fell over his left shoulder.

Like Tomorrow, Marcus had locs. They were long and brown, and fell over his shoulders. He was definitely a sight to behold.

She watched from the bed as he got completely naked, revealing his less than adequate package. Tomorrow's smile quickly turned to a disappointed frown when Marcus walked over to her, barely swinging any length.

What the fuck does he think he's gonna do with that? she thought.

"Nina, I've been waiting for this since the first day I saw you in Alexandria. You were looking fly as hell strutting across the street to your BMW," Marcus said licking his lips.

"Oh really?" Tomorrow replied slowly unbuttoning her blouse.

"Hell yeah." He grabbed his miniature manhood. "Come closer."

Marcus did as he was told and walked closer to Tomorrow. She gently grabbed his locs and pulled him onto her as she lay back on the bed. He closed his eyes and kissed her softly.

Her kisses had him floating on cloud nine and he didn't want to come back down.

"Here. Put this on," Tomorrow whispered.

She handed him a condom and he quickly put it on. He slid inside of her and drifted off to heaven. Her pussy was like none he had ever experienced. Marcus rapidly pumped in an attempt to beat the rush. He knew he wasn't the type of dude to last all night, so he wanted to get in as many pumps as he could.

Tomorrow rolled her eyes and lay stiff as a board. It was almost as if she wasn't even there. Marcus seemed to be having the time of his life, and meanwhile, she was nearly dozing off.

I guess you really CAN'T trust the big feet theory, Tomorrow thought to herself.

Marcus abruptly stopped pumping and Tomorrow secretly hoped that he had climaxed already so that she could get the hell out of that house. His eyes rolled to the back of his head and he fell over.

"Ughhhh. I don't feel so good." Marcus groaned in pain.

"You aight boo?" Tomorrow asked, rubbing his back.

"No, I'm dizzy and I think I'm gonna..." Marcus' sentence was cut short.

He immediately fell unconscious.

"Finally! What the fuck took your fat ass so long?" Tomorrow snapped.

She kicked Marcus from the bed onto the floor and ran over to her Prada duffel bag. She retrieved a rope from the bag and bound both of his arms to the bed post and waited for him to wake up.

A few hours later, Marcus was awakened by an intense pain.

"What the fuck is wrong with you, bitch?" He screamed while looking down at the place where his manhood once resided.

"Shut the fuck up, you fuckin' clown. Be lucky I cut that shit off, you should be embarrassed."

"Nina, I swear I'm gonna fuck you up!" Marcus screamed in pain.

"Nigga, I did you a favor. I didn't even know dick came in that size anymore. Did you forget to super-size, nigga?" Tomorrow taunted.

Tomorrow wiggled Marcus' dick in front of his face.

"Ewww, look at it. It looks like a baby thumb." Tomorrow giggled.

"Bitch, are you crazy? I gotta get to a fuckin' hospital before I lose too much blood."

"Nigga, you don't get it do you?" Tomorrow laughed. "You aint making it out of here alive."

"Let me go, Nina Douglass!" Marcus yelled.

Tomorrow laughed uncontrollably. She had to give him an A for effort, but there was no way she would be caught. Marcus could scream for help, but it was no use.

His attempt to scream her name aloud so that someone would hear it was quite clever, but the problem was her name wasn't Nina.

She went over to her duffel bag and pulled out her Dexter Russell.

"Now, this won't hurt a bit," she whispered.

Tomorrow took her knife and swiftly slit Marcus from ear to ear. She wiped the blood residue onto his bed sheets and put Dexter back into her bag.

She quickly headed for the door but remembered that she had forgotten one thing.

She ran back to the room and planted a kiss on Marcus' forehead.

"Sweet Dreams."

CHAPTER

~ 8 ~

*S*pring break arrived and school was out for a couple of weeks. This was Legacy's chance to finally speak to Kane without any interruptions. She woke up early Sunday morning and called his cell phone.

She could tell that he had pressed the ignore button when the phone immediately went to voicemail.

I'm tired of this shit. Looks like I'mma have to **make** *this nigga talk to me.*

She drove over to Kane's house and pounded on the door. When no one answered, she leaned over and peeked through his mail slot.

"Open up! I know you're in there," Legacy insisted.

After five minutes of knocking, an older black woman came to the door. She was the spitting image of Kane and wore a blue robe with pink foam rollers in her hair.

She peered at Legacy as a Black & Mild hung from her dark lips. She held a can of 211 in her left hand and her right hand was on her hip.

"Girl, have you lost your damn mind? Banging on my door like you the goddamn police!"

Legacy froze. She normally had something smart to say, but the lady that stood before her had an intimidating look.

"Umm, is—is Kane home?"

"Who are you?"

"My name is Legacy and I was wondering if I could see him, because I have something important tell him."

The woman grew concerned. She stepped outside the screen door and slammed it behind her.

"Like what?" she asked.

Legacy was petrified. She wasn't sure whether or not she should reveal her sham of a pregnancy, but knew that there was a possibility it would get Kane to speak to her.

"Are you his mother?"

"That I am!"

"Well I just wanted to see if he was going on any spring break trips this year."

"Are you that girl with the black BMW that be creepin' over here on the late night?"

Legacy was shocked. Her heart fell to the floor and sent her mind into a frenzy.

Tomorrow! She thought to herself.

She was unsure if Mishon, Tomorrow, or both were stabbing her in the back, but she had to get to the bottom of it.

"Yeah, that's me," she lied.

"Well, let me tell you like I told my son. I'm the only sinner in this house. This ain't no muthafuckin' hood house. With your lying ass! You know damn well you didn't come all the way over here to talk about some damn spring break trip!"

"I swear I did."

"Little girl, do you think I'm stupid? That's what's wrong with y'all young bucks now. Y'all think y'all so sneaky and don't know how to run shit. Now why would you drive to someone's house to ask a question like that? When all you got to do is call, text, or take your silly ass on FaceBook. Now who you think you foolin'?"

"Well, is Kane here?" Legacy coughed.

His mother flicked her cigar over her shoulder ensuring that the ashes blew in Legacy's face.

"No! Now get your fast ass off my porch."

Legacy quickly walked away from Kane's house and headed for her car. The intensity of the situation along with the smoke from his mother's cigar made it hard for her to breathe. As soon as she got back in the car, she frantically searched for her inhaler. She was having a mini panic attack.

"I thought I brought my purse with me." She coughed.

Legacy became frantic when her head started spinning. When her sight turned blurry, she knew she needed to get help soon. She jumped out of the car only to find Kane's mother standing there holding her purse.

"You forgot your purse on my porch. Must've sat it down when you were peeping in my mail slot." Kane's mother smirked.

Legacy snatched it out of her hand and emptied the contents on the trunk of her car.

"Come on, where are you?" She pondered while shaking the life out of the bag.

The inhaler was the last thing to fall out. She took three

long pulls and sat on the curb to collect herself.

"Thank you," Legacy wheezed.

"Girl, bring your ass in this house and get some damn water. Got the nerve to be peeping in somebody's house with some damn asthma! You're a smooth criminal alright."

Legacy did as she was told, but she didn't forget about the unfinished business that she had to attend to.

Kane's mother handed Legacy a glass of water and sat directly across from her. She shook her head and laughed. She couldn't believe that her son had these little girls going crazy over him.

After being around Legacy for a few moments, Kane's mother knew she had to be the little girl who Kane always complained about, but there was just one thing that didn't sit right with her.

"Um, I thought you said you drove that black BMW?"

CHAPTER

~ 9 ~

Tomorrow met up with Mishon for breakfast at the Table Talk Restaurant. The Table Talk was the place where all the local college kids hung out in their spare time, and the food was delicious.

Tomorrow knew that Mishon was planning their annual trip, because she had done it every year since they were in the tenth grade.

She looked at the goofy expression on Mishon's face and could tell that she was really happy about this year's trip. Tomorrow sighed. She wasn't really in the mood for another spring break activity, but since she desperately needed a getaway, she figured she'd just suck it up and try to enjoy herself.

"Let me guess, I'm here to hear details about going on this vacation," Tomorrow said matter-of-factly.

"Bitch, you know me too well. Besides, we need it."

"I guess."

"Tomorrow, what's wrong with you? Ever since I discovered that bruise on your ribs, you been acting kinda fishy. Now, I thought I was your girl. You supposed to tell me everything."

Mishon was right. She knew Tomorrow was concealing something, but she just couldn't put her finger on it.

"Plus, you never really did tell me how that happened."

"I've been stressed the fuck out lately. I swear I'mma tell you, but now is not the right time. Trust me." Tomorrow gritted her teeth.

The last thing she wanted to do was discuss how she got that bruise on her ribs. In fact, she wanted to forget that the incident had ever happened and hoped Mishon would just eventually let it go.

"Okaaay, well let's change the subject. How about Ocean City this time? Brandon hooked up a condominium on the ocean front," Mishon bragged.

"Really? That sounds goood. We gon' have so much fun. Plus, I need a place to relax and gather my thoughts."

"Girl, who you telling?"

Brandon walked into the restaurant and found where the girls were sitting.

"What's good, Tomorrow?" he spoke as he sat down, leaning over to give Mishon a kiss.

"Nuthin' much. I heard you hooked us up with a spot in Ocean City."

"Yeah, my girl, well you know how she is, always gotta spend a nigga's money up."

"Haha, yeah, she's known for that."

Mishon smacked Brandon's leg jokingly.

"I do not." She laughed.

All conversation at the table ceased when Kane walked into the diner. He spotted Tomorrow sitting with Mishon and Brandon. He hadn't had a chance to speak to Tomorrow since the night that she snuck out of his back door. Even during the incident at Trell's party, the two hadn't really spoken. He wasn't sure if things were cool between them, but he decided to go speak anyway.

"Hey everybody, what's good?" Kane asked.

Mishon and Tomorrow waved hoping that Brandon wouldn't pop off.

"Hey Kane, have a seat. Come eat with us," Brandon offered.

It took a minute, but Kane eventually pulled up a seat. He didn't want any more problems and was curious as to what Brandon had to say. Mishon and Tomorrow stared at each with a look that said Oh my god.

"What you doin' for spring break?" Brandon asked.

"Well, nothing serious. Why? What's good?"

"We all headed to O.C. for a few days. Wanna roll?"

Tomorrow and Mishon each took a long deep breath because they had no clue what Brandon would do, but they were glad that he was willing to make amends.

"I mean, if it's cool with y'all." Kane said.

"Listen, I ain't got no quarrels with you. The past is the past, but understand, Mishon is all I have, and if I lose her, I'mma be all fucked up. So that shit you pulled had me fucked up and I had to set the shit straight, I wouldn't be who I am if I didn't. But I'm good now. You dig?"

"Word." Kane nodded in agreement.

"The offer is open. You cool with my people, so I'mma try and be cool with you. We can let bygones be bygones."

"Aight, koo." Kane agreed.

"Now let's eat."

Mishon was glad to have Kane along for the relaxing getaway, but Tomorrow showed no emotion when Kane decided to attend. Tomorrow wasn't really sure if she was done with Kane sexually, but she knew that there was no way that they'd be anything more than just friends with benefits. Hopefully, she could get through this trip without having to kill him.

CHAPTER

~ 10 ~

Legacy had finally come up with a plan to confront her Tomorrow situation, and now it was finally time to officially put her plan into action.

She was draped in all black and accessorized with black hoop earrings to add a feminine touch. Legacy's ninja inspired outfit was simply a ploy to keep a low profile while she executed her plan. She had to make sure that she was unnoticed, or everything she had in store would backfire with dire consequences. Although she was willing to do whatever it took to make sure that Tomorrow would just go away, how could she explain being caught breaking and entering?

She drove to Tomorrow's house and parked adjacently. She waited patiently outside in her car scoping out the house with black binoculars. She noticed that the kitchen light was the only light on in the house.

"I'mma get this bitch," she whispered. "She obviously don't know who she messin wit."

She watched as Tomorrow's mother Janet frequently walked in and out of the room carry dishes and trays of food.

"What the fuck is she doin'? Is that lobster?"

Legacy crept around to the back of Tomorrow's house to see what Janet was up to. As she got closer, she heard champagne flutes clicking, and she could also hear a group of people talking about interior design school.

She raced back to her car and called Tomorrow's house, but dialed *67 first hoping she wouldn't pick up.

"Praise the Lord. Who's calling?"

"Umm, wait! What did you just say?"

"I said Praise the Lord. Who's calling!?"

Legacy wanted to laugh so hard, but she knew she had to keep her composure in order to complete the mission. She covered her mouth with her hand until the laughter ceased.

"May I speak to Tomorrow please?"

"Sorry, you've just missed her. She stepped out for a while, but can I take a message?"

"Sure, can you please tell her Lisa called? Thanks."

"Okay baby, goodbye."

Legacy got out the car again and raced back across the street. This time she was going to break in. It was a good thing that Tomorrow lived in an end unit townhome, otherwise her mission would've been impossible.

She crawled up to the window located on the side of the house and slid in. Legacy tiptoed across the marble floor and up the staircase. She walked down the hall and saw two

94

rooms on her left. She wasn't sure which one belonged to Tomorrow, but judging by the beware sign on the first door, she knew that had to be it. She walked in and quickly shut the door behind her.

"Whew! That took a lot out of me," she whispered.

Legacy pulled the inhaler out of her pocket and took two small puffs.

She was taken aback by the sight she beheld. Tomorrow's room was flawless; everything had a specific place and Legacy was almost afraid to even walk in the room unnoticed.

There were at least three or four dozen color coded shoes aligned against the wall. The queen canopy bed was made without any wrinkles. In the closet were clothes that hung on only red velvet hangers.

She scoured through Tomorrow's immaculate room making sure that she put things back just the way she found them.

"Okay, this uptight bitch has OCD really bad." Legacy chuckled.

She walked around carefully and noticed a door that led to Tomorrow's own personal bathroom.

"This bitch even got a bathroom inside her room? I can't stand this uppity ho!" she said with spite in her voice.

Legacy had to go in. She knew that a lot of secrets could be found while snooping through someone's belongings, especially in a bathroom. Her first reaction was to head for the medicine cabinet. She noticed that Tomorrow had three prescription bottles with names of medications that she couldn't pronounce. She took out her iPhone and wrote down the three names.

"I wonder what the fuck this shit is? That bitch probably got a prescription for crabs or something," Legacy joked.

She looked down and noticed an empty bottle in the trash can.

"Just what the fuck I need," she said while putting the bottle in her hoodie.

Janet was still entertaining friends, which made it really easy for Legacy to slip back out of the house undetected.

Finally, Legacy had accomplished something without screwing it up. The excitement from breaking into Tomorrow's house made her feel untouchable.

***

"Thanks for agreeing to go out with me, Tomorrow. I know it was a little unconventional, but I really wanted to connect with you."

"No problem. My mother has been raving about you since forever. I knew eventually she'd try to play mother match-maker."

"I love Sister Robinson. She's always on point, and you can see the love of God shining through her."

Tomorrow sat across from Micah at the Bread & Chocolate cafe in Old Town Alexandria.

She was nervous because she had never been on a real date before, not like this. She couldn't believe that she had actually agreed to go out on a date with the son of a deacon, but the urge to please her mother was almost as strong as the urge she had to kill.

"Yes, everyone loves my mother." Tomorrow faked a smile.

Micah was poised. He was a tall with a caramel complexion, broad shoulders and a stance that said he was important. He spoke with such confidence and charisma and there was something special about him that Tomorrow couldn't quite touch.

"So, Tomorrow, what have you been up to? I hear you have a few things going on with your music?"

"Well, I'm still in school but I'm working on writing my first book and a neo soul mixtape."

"Wow, congrats. That's definitely a good thing. Let me know when you release them, especially the mixtape. I'd love to hear it. You always did have a beautiful voice." Micah smiled.

His smile was brilliant and perfectly complimented the rest of his beautiful face.

Tomorrow couldn't help but secretly lust for him. She knew she would never go there, but it didn't hurt to fantasize about it.

"Thanks. I guess it was all the Sunday Morning Worship over at His Light AME." Tomorrow laughed.

"Speaking of, why haven't I seen you in those choir stands lately?" Micah inquired.

"I don't know. I kinda just lost the inspiration to sing."

"But you have enough inspiration to do your mixtape?"

"Here we go."

"No, I'm not gonna preach to you. You already know what you need to do. Stop holding back your gifts and let that light shine for the Lord."

"One of these days, I will." Tomorrow sighed.

Tomorrow watched as Micah took a sip of his caramel mocha latte. His lips were so full and juicy that she couldn't help but imagine all of the things that she'd allow him to do with them.

Puddles slowly formed in her panties, and she knew she'd have to get out of there soon. She definitely didn't want to be responsible for seducing a future pastor, let alone killing one.

"Just don't wait too long."

Tomorrow looked down at her phone and noticed the

time.

"Hey, I gotta go. Something um, just came up."

"So soon? Was it something I said?" Micah questioned.

"No, I just... I just gotta go. Rain check." Tomorrow stood up from the table.

"Tomorrow, it's on my heart to say this to you. You have to stop running from your problems. You're a part of something that's much bigger than you, and if you don't face it head on, you're gonna get swallowed up in it," Micah spoke sternly.

He gently grabbed Tomorrow's hand, but she pulled away.

"I'm sorry, I just have to go."

Tomorrow quickly exited the cafe. She had to get far away from Micah before she did the unspeakable. He rushed to pay for the check and then hurriedly ran after her, calling out her name.

"Wait!" Micah yelled. He saw Tomorrow stop and he ran over to her before she got into her car.

"Micah. Look, I'm sorry, I just cant—"

Her words were stopped by Micah's kiss to her lips. His kiss sent tingles through her body and she wanted to tear his clothes off right there at the car. She didn't understand why he had done something like that, but she wished that he hadn't. If he knew who she was and what she was capable of, he would've been trying to get as far away from her as possible. She was turning into someone she didn't even know, and she wasn't able to control it.

"Why did you do that?" Tomorrow sighed.

"I'm so sorry. I really shouldn't have done that. I let my flesh get the best of me and I apologize." Micah sounded apologetic.

"It's okay. I just wasn't expecting that. Especially from

someone like you."

"Why? I'm a man of God, but at the end of the day, I'm still a man. I'm human. It's definitely a work in progress."

"I can account to that." Tomorrow laughed.

"Yeah, and besides, you know they say temptation is like the kiss of death."

"What did you just say?" Tomorrow's eyes grew wide with fear.

"I said temptation is like the kiss of death."

"I gotta go."

"What? Why?"

"I just gotta go," Tomorrow insisted.

"Okay," Micah sadly replied.

Tomorrow rushed into her car and fumbled for the keys. She had to get far away from Micah before she corrupted him, or did something worse. He watched as she frantically drove off down the street.

What is it about her?

***

"Who the fuck was in my room?"

Tomorrow could smell the scent of cheap perfume lingering throughout her bedroom. Things just didn't feel right, and she knew that someone had been there.

She looked around and saw that one of her Manolo Blahnik BB Leopard-Print Ponies had been slightly moved.

Tomorrow generally kept all of her shoes at a 45 degree angle,and now they were no longer in the spot that she had put them. Who had been in her room?

Seeing her things out of place sent Tomorrow into a rage. She hated when things were out of order. She hurriedly bent down and placed her pumps in their correct position.

It was bad enough that she had to end her date early so

that she wouldn't kill Micah, but now somebody had been in her room without her permission. She snapped.

"$800 fucking shoes!" Tomorrow screamed.

She threw her duffel bag against the bathroom door, revealing all of its contents. Her blood stained Dexter Russell butcher knife peered from the bag, reminding Tomorrow of her last offense. She knew she had to get a grip.

Tomorrow paced back and forth trying to calm herself down. She wasn't due for another dose of lithium for at least another hour or so, but she could feel the effects of her disorder slowly seeping in. She instantly felt strong urges to fuck and kill simultaneously. Those feelings quickly overwhelmed her, and she broke down.

"Why me? Why is it always fucking me?" Tomorrow screamed.

She dropped to her knees and began to sob uncontrollably. Tomorrow had so much that she needed to release from within. Keeping up appearances had proved harder than she had bargained for.

Tomorrow was many things, but perfect was definitely not one of them. It's true, killing had become a guilty pleasure of hers, but keeping it a secret was the hardest thing she had ever done.

It all started from the compulsion to finish her book. She needed to research uncharted territory and thought that becoming her own case study would be perfect.

Tomorrow had been diagnosed with bipolar II disorder at the age of ten. It had only been discovered after her mother Janet noticed that her newfound erratic behavior had gotten way out of control.

In the beginning, Janet refused to see it. Her daughter had suffered a traumatic experience while living in Chicago, and because of that, she overlooked Tomorrow's disorder as her simply being rebellious and acting out. But after Janet came home to find Tomorrow stabbing her headless dolls with a butcher knife, she knew she had to get her some help.

Janet walked down the hall and headed towards her daughter's bedroom. She noticed that Tomorrow was particularly quiet and decided to check in on her. She looked in and could only see her daughter from behind. She noticed that Tomorrow was standing over her dolls with her hands raised up high. Janet gasped when she realized that her daughter was holding a butcher knife.

"Die muthafuckas!" young Tomorrow screamed.

"TOMORROW! WHAT ARE YOU DOING?"

Hearing her mother's voice shocked Tomorrow back into reality. She turned and looked at Janet with her big puppy dog eyes and began to cry.

"Mommy, you scared me. I was just playing with them, and then I just got so angry. I had to hurt them, Mommy, just like they hurt me."

Janet ran over to her daughter and pried the knife from her hands. She held her tightly and cried.

"Baby, don't you ever do that again, okay? Mommy's gonna get you the help you need."

"What's wrong with me, Mommy?"

"Baby, you're perfect. Mommy is gonna make sure of it. Don't ever let anybody tell you anything different, you hear me? You're perfect!" Janet cried.

"Okay, Mommy."

"If you don't remember anything else, baby, remember that it's all about the image. You can be whatever you wanna be. It's always about how it appears, that's just the way it is. Do you understand?"

"I think so. I'm perfect because I say so, right Mommy?"

"Exactly baby, exactly!"

At one time, Tomorrow had complete control over her

disorder. There were times where her mood would dramatically fluctuate, but for the most part, as long as she took her medicine, things were smooth sailing. That is, until she started to write her book.

The more she studied herself and the people around her, the more intrigued she became, especially once she realized the extent of her disorder and just how far she could really sink into psychosis. She had researched many cases of people with bipolar II and realized that allowing her sexual urges to manifest to the limits could be just the thing she needed to take her book over the top and get the best seller that she had always dreamed of. Besides, her mother wanted the best, and she was going to give it to her one way or another.

The problem was Tomorrow no longer had control over her urges. She had become a serial killer with no real grip on reality, and it was only a matter of time before things spun dangerously out of control.

Amidst her fit of rage, Tomorrow looked down and noticed something shining from the floor. She immediately knew who the culprit was.

"Oh, this bitch is bold as fuck. I hope she found what she was looking for, because once I get a hold of her, it's a wrap!"

CHAPTER

~ 11 ~

They walked into their two-bedroom ocean front condominium and immedi ately noticed the breathtaking view of the beach.

Tomorrow and Mishon ran to the balcony and gasped at just how beautiful the scenery looked from their location.

"OMG, do you see this view?" Tomorrow whispered.

She closed her eyes and allowed the breeze to tickle her face. She knew that there was absolutely nothing that would ruin this vacation for her.

"My baby did his thing. He told me that The Sea Watch would be the perfect spot in Ocean City," Mishon bragged.

"Let's go look at the bedrooms." Tomorrow pulled Mishon by the arm and led her into the house.

"Y'all are like kids in a fucking candy store." Brandon laughed as he walked into the condo's den.

"Oh, this is definitely gonna be the men's area," Brandon's friend Chris said, following behind him.

The den was completely laid. It was the perfect place for the men to dwell. Brandon and Chris found two cozy, chocolate brown love seats and immediately got comfortable. They admired the huge plasma TV that hung from the wall and assumed that the room would strictly be for watching basketball.

"No, fuck that. That's serving as the extra bedroom unless somebody plan to sleep on the couch or floor around this joint," Mishon exclaimed as she walked into the den behind the guys.

"Don't you see these two beds in here? That means it's an extra bedroom, and since we don't know if Kane is actually coming, y'all gotta hold off on the man cave," she continued.

"Either way. It'll be a man cave," Brandon joked.

"So how we plan on doing this rooming thing?" Chris inquired as he watched Tomorrow pass by the den and head back towards the balcony.

"Well, there's two bedrooms and this den. Plus, there's a queen size pull out bed in the living room, but I'm not sure if you want that, cuz I know you like your privacy."

"Most definitely. I need like no noise when I'm tryna relax," Chis responded.

"So of course me and my boo got a room. I already put our stuff down in the master bedroom, and the bed is huge. My girl Tomorrow is gonna be in the guest bedroom, which also has a queen size bed by the way," Mishon hinted. "Maybe if you're nice, she'll let you room with her."

Chris didn't respond. He was too busy admiring Tomorrow's frame to pay attention to what Mishon was saying.

He had been crushing on Tomorrow for a while, but never really said anything. She seemed like she already had a lot going on and he wasn't one to chase a female. He never had to.

Chris was 6'3" and 215 pounds of chocolate bliss. He had a low cut Caesar, and his waves equally matched those of the ocean that rested in front of them. He was sexy, and he knew he could have any woman that he wanted.

He and Brandon were childhood friends, almost like brothers. When Brandon started dating Mishon over a year ago, he put Chris on to Tomorrow, but it never manifested into anything more than acquaintances. Both were always too busy doing their own thing, but perhaps now was the perfect time for the two to really connect.

"Cough, cough nigga! Don't you hear me talking to yo' ass?" Mishon exclaimed.

She watched as Chris stared at Tomorrow and smiled. She had a little matchmaker plan of her own, but she definitely wouldn't tell Tomorrow that.

Mishon always thought that Tomorrow and Chris would make a good couple, but they were both overly consumed with their own lives to even look at each other as anything more than friends. She could hear Tomorrow now: *Nah, girl. We're koo but we just don't connect like that.*

Mishon laughed to herself as she thought about how Tomorrow refused to talk to Chris, but ended up fucking with someone like Kane. Kane was fine, but he was definitely not Chris.

"I hear you. I'll see what's up with her," Chris responded.

Tomorrow sat in a chair on the condo's balcony and enjoyed the view. She didn't know how she had managed to find her way back outdoors. It was almost as if she was drawn to the sounds of the ocean. There was something about the water that calmed her spirit, as if everything in the world was perfect if only for that moment.

She closed her eyes and inhaled. She almost wanted to cry, but she knew she wasn't alone. So much fell on her spirit, and she knew that eventually she'd have to release it. Now just wasn't the time.

"Do you mind if I join you?" Chris asked as he slid the balcony's door open and poked his head out.

"Not at all," Tomorrow responded.

She watched Chris intensely as he sat down in the chair beside her. She wondered why he wasn't with Brandon, enjoying the flat screen.

"So, how you been?" Chris asked, making small talk.

"I'm okay. Glad to be here on this getaway. I really needed it." Tomorrow exhaled.

"Huh man. I feel you on that one. Shit can get kinda stressful back home, so it's always good to just get away and clear your mind sometimes. Besides, this shit is beautiful. I could stay here forever."

"Most def. Almost like some fairytale type shit, right?" Tomorrow giggled.

"Exactly. Well, we have a lil' dilemma. It seems as if I may need a roommate. You know anyone?" Chris inquired.

"Yeah. I'm sure Brandon and Mishon wouldn't mind you squeezing in between them." Tomorrow laughed aloud.

"Oh, you got jokes for days, right?" Chris joined in with the laughter.

"I don't mind you rooming with me. Just don't try nothing. I'm a good girl."

"So I've heard," Chris said sarcastically.

"What does that mean?"

"Look, you don't have to be perfect around me, shawty. We all got flaws. Some more than others, but nonetheless, we all got 'em. I ain't tryna wife you–or one night you. You know how we do, right?"

"Yeah. I do. Strictly platonic."

"Yeah. We both got our own shit going on, and for whatever reason, right now we here. So let's make the best of it."

"True."

"Now, if you feel the need to rub a nigga down, I won't be mad at that either," Chris joked.

"Mmm. Anything's possible, right?"

Tomorrow stood up and headed towards the sliding door.

"I'll be back," she said.

"I know."

Tomorrow walked into the condo and exhaled heavily. Chris could always do that to her. She couldn't stand the fact that he had such an effect on her. He seemed almost unaffected by all of the games and seduction that came with Tomorrow, and yet, he was still willing to play. But he was only willing to play in his own way. It was as if Chris was the male version of her, and she didn't know how to handle it.

He made Tomorrow nervous, a feeling that she had never felt. Because of that, she never wanted to pursue anything with him. It would be all too real in a world that she had completely faked for so long.

It was almost as if he already knew her. Chris could read her mind and she wasn't used to the tables being turned. Tomorrow generally avoided him at all costs, and now she was going to be stuck with him for an entire week.

Tomorrow knew she had to avoid him. Her newfound desire to kill overwhelmed her. Her medicine had her levelheaded, but not enough to stop the urges to commit murder. She had already dodged Micah, and now she knew she would have to dodge Chris too.

She actually liked Chris and didn't want any harm to come to him, especially not by her own hands.

What am I gonna do?

Lost in her thoughts, she heard a knock at the door that snapped her back into reality.

Tomorrow walked to the front door and saw Kane standing there with a smile from ear to ear. Despite the fact that they had sporadically seen each other on campus and at the Table Talk restaurant, Kane and Tomorrow's contact had become quite limited. They hadn't been in contact since the night of the party, and after Brandon had embarrassed him in front of everyone, she really didn't have the desire to speak to him at all. However, seeing him at the door seemed to some-what get her excited.

That is, until she looked to the left and realized that Kane wasn't alone. He had Legacy with him and she didn't have a pleasant look on her face.

This bitch better not ruin my trip!

She hoped that Legacy wouldn't be there. She wanted this trip to be relaxing and peaceful, but she had a feeling that Legacy would never allow it to go down like that.

"Hey, what's up Tomorrow," Kane said excitedly.

"Kane," Tomorrow said flatly.

"Is Kane the only one you see?" Legacy said with an attitude.

That's strike one bitch, Tomorrow thought. "Surprised to see you here, Legacy," she sneered. "Mishon, look who's here. It's Kane and *Legaaacccy!*" Tomorrow sang in delight.

Mishon walked into the living room with an indescrib-able look on her face. She looked as if she could choke the shit out of Kane for even considering bringing Legacy on the trip. She was even more confused at how Legacy's hooptie had managed to make it so far.

"Kane, really though, nigga?" Mishon said with an attitude.

"Long story."

Kane knew that he was wrong for bringing Legacy on the trip, but he didn't have any choice. Legacy was the only way he would've been able to make the trip. Besides, he didn't want to miss any chance to spend a little time with Tomorrow.

"Mishon, can we go to the balcony and talk, please?" Legacy questioned.

"For what, bitch? What are you even doing here?"

"Look, I don't want no problems. I'm here to have a good time like everybody else. Can we just talk, please?" Legacy was sincere.

Legacy realized that she had wrongly accused Mishon of sleeping with Kane. She felt bad for making such a scene, especially when Tomorrow was the one who she should have really been keeping an eye on.

"Fine, but don't try nothing, bitch. I will flip yo' ass into the ocean," Mishon warned as she walked towards the balcony's sliding doors. Legacy walked out behind her.

Chris walked back in and noticed that everyone was silent.

"Why everybody so quiet?" he questioned.

"We're just trying to make sure that no one accidentally gets pushed into the deep blue," Tomorrow snickered.

Nobody else thought it was funny. With Mishon's temper, there was definitely a possibility that Legacy could go flying head first into the salt water.

Mishon sat down and pulled out one of her Newports. She knew that this conversation would definitely call for a cigarette.

"So," Mishon began. "What is it that you wanna talk

about?"

"Look, I just wanna apologize for all this shit that's been going on. I got so caught up in Kane's shit, and I blamed you for something that wasn't even going down, and I'm sorry."

Mishon didn't say a word. She just looked at Legacy with unaffected eyes. She honestly just wanted to punch Legacy in the face, but she decided she'd just let it go. She was on a nice vacation and would do anything she could to ensure that the trip went smoothly, even if that meant making up with Legacy.

"I know you're mad, Shon, but I really am sorry. We been best friends since the eighth grade, and I don't wanna end that over some sorry ass nigga. I know you ain't fuck Kane. I was just going crazy cuz he keep taking me through so much dumb shit."

Mishon hesitated before speaking. She could tell that Legacy was sympathetic and hoped that she'd finally get it together.

"Aight. We good. But don't be starting that dumb ass shit. I don't want Kane, I got a good man, and I don't need nobody fucking up my shit. I ain't a ho, and I don't appreciate you trying to insinuate that I was."

"I know, I'm sorry. Let's just put this shit behind us. Besides, I got some deep ass shit to tell you anyway."

"Save it, ho," Mishon warned.

"I thought we was tryna put this shit behind us," Legacy whined.

Legacy expected everything to be cool after she apologized, but Mishon really just didn't trust her anymore. She had been searching for a reason to get out of their friendship anyway, and now that she had a legitimate reason, she didn't want to tread backwards.

"Look now, I'mma be civil to your ass for the sake of

TOMORROW'S SEDUCTION: KISS OF DEATH

this trip. When we get back, we can talk about trying to get our friendship back on track or whatever the fuck it's gonna be, but for now, I just wanna enjoy my vacation. So don't be starting no shit."

"I'm good. Like I said, I just wanna enjoy myself too," Legacy responded. *And make sure I get even with that bitch, Tomorrow.*

CHAPTER

~ 12 ~

The Ocean City trip seemed to be running smoothly and everyone was happy about that. For two days, everyone had been enjoying their fun in the sun worry free. So far, no one had any problems and it seemed as if everyone would have a stress free vacation.

After an exciting day at the beach, everyone came back to the condo to relax. Mishon and Tomorrow decided to make dinner because everyone had worked up an appetite.

Tomorrow cooked jerk chicken and rice while Mishon cooked the cabbage and skillet cornbread. They all sat down at the dining room table and enjoyed the meal.

"Damn, this shit is good, baby. Y'all did that!" Brandon

said licking his fingers.

"Are we gonna get this special treatment all week?" Chris chimed in.

"Hell nah. We on vacation too. Shit, the rest of the week, y'all on y'all own. Better order a pizza or get some food from the boardwalk. Nigga, what you think this is?" Mishon jokingly sassed.

"Oh, so y'all tryna spoil a nigga, then gonna snatch it away. That's fucked up," Kane joined in.

"That ain't the only thing that's 'bout to get snatched," Legacy added.

Everyone ignored Legacy's slick comment. That wasn't the first time she had made an off the wall remark. She seemed overly eager to say little things, especially when it involved Tomorrow.

Unfortunately, Tomorrow was unaffected by Legacy's snide remarks. She was too busy trying to rid her own demons and decided to pay Legacy no attention, unless of course she decided to get out of hand.

Mishon shot Legacy an angry look to let her know to pipe down with the comments.

"Who wants drinks?" Tomorrow yelled, pulling out the Jose Cuervo and the shot glasses.

"Hell yeah, bitch. Let's get this party started right!" Mishon responded. She pulled out two blunts and a lighter from her pocket.

"My type of party," Chris added while pulling two blunts from his own pocket.

"I can't drink," Legacy said, holding her stomach.

Mishon and Tomorrow snickered. They couldn't believe that Legacy was still keeping up with the whole fake pregnancy thing.

"Why not?" Brandon asked.

He knew the answer. He just thought it was incredibly funny that Legacy refused to just give it a rest.

"Yeah, Legacy, why not?" Tomorrow laughed.

Legacy rolled her eyes. She had an urge to give Tomorrow a piece of her mind, but decided that it wasn't the right time. She was going to fuck up Tomorrow's whole world, and she would enjoy every minute of it.

"Because I'm pregnant."

"Oh wow. Man, I didn't know your girl was pregnant, congrats!" Chris said, smiling at Kane.

Mishon and Tomorrow burst into laughter.

"What?" Chris was confused.

"Yeah, what the fuck y'all hoes laughing at?" Legacy was offended.

"Bitch, you still going on with this shit? Let it go. Get a fucking beanie baby and move on with your life!" Mishon laughed.

"I am pregnant. I went and heard the heartbeat and everything!" Legacy screamed.

"You're crazy as hell!" Kane finally said.

Everyone laughed.

"You're fucking bonkers, bitch. You are not pregnant. Stop telling people that shit!" He yelled.

"Oh, trust me. I ain't the crazy one in this bunch." Legacy looked at Tomorrow with a sinister smirk.

Tomorrow just laughed. Legacy tried so hard to play the game, but if she only knew. She had definitely picked the wrong one to go to war with. Tomorrow wasn't sure exactly what Legacy knew, but she figured that she had to know something. Her generic bad girl impression said it all. Tomorrow refused to let Legacy see her sweat. She had been up against worse opponents, so to her, Legacy was nothing but a lightweight. She was going to have some real fun teaching her who the true queen of deception was.

Tomorrow filled her shot glass with Jose Cuervo and immediately took it back. She felt her chest become warm and tingly. A few more of those, along with a nice spliff, and Tomorrow would be floating on cloud nine.

"Bottoms up," Tomorrow said before chugging down shots number two, three, and four.

Everyone else except Legacy followed in the partaking of the shots.

"Well, I'mma call it a night since everybody drinking and smoking. I'll see y'all in the morning." Legacy got up from the table and made her way to the den.

"Good. Now pass one of those blunts in this direction," Tomorrow insisted.

Chris passed his blunt to Tomorrow. She noticed that the tip of the blunt was wet, but she still indulged.

"Damn, you and your juicy ass lips drenched the whole damn blunt." Tomorrow laughed.

"Aye, you ain't gotta smoke my shit. Me and my juicy ass lips can smoke this alone."

"I'm just saying."

"So you think I got some juicy ass lips, huh?" Chris laughed.

Kane stared at Tomorrow and Chris. He could clearly see that they had some sexual chemistry between them. Although he would never admit it, he was a bit jealous that Tomorrow was so interested in what Chris was doing, but she had barely spoken a word to him.

After smoking and taking shots, everyone was feeling lovely. Kane was horny and wanted Tomorrow so badly. He knew that she was the only one who could fuck him like he really needed, but there was no way that it was going to happen, especially once he found out that Chris would be rooming with

116

Tomorrow.

That nigga coulda slept on that sofa bed, he thought to himself before getting up from the table.

"Nigga, you gone?" Chris asked Kane.

Kane grabbed his dick and looked down.

"Yeah, a nigga gotta go—go let off some steeeeeam." Kane laughed at his slurred words.

Good luck with that, nigga, ain't no pussy better than mine. Tomorrow giggled to herself before taking her final shot.

They all watched as Kane struggled to make it to the bedroom.

Finally, Kane stumbled into the den and got into the bed with Legacy. He figured that at this point, any pussy was better than none.

"Damn, dude 'bout to get it in, huh?" Brandon joked from the living room.

"Hey, well you know what they say: pregnant pussy is the best pussy," Chris joined in.

"I wonder what they say about fake pregnancy pussy," Tomorrow blurted out.

Everyone laughed.

"I'm 'bout to call it a night myself. I got that never been pregnant pussy and I know my baby wanna try it, right boo?" Mishon giggled.

"Oh, you know it." Brandon rubbed his hands together.

Mishon and Brandon excused themselves from the living room and walked into the master bedroom. Tomorrow felt her body tense when she noticed that she was alone with Chris. The fact that she had a few drinks in her belly only made her more nervous.

"So what kinda pussy you got, Tomorrow?" Chris seductively asked.

"I got that I know you really want it but ain't never

gonna get it pussy." Tomorrow laughed.

"Interesting."

"Indeed it is," Tomorrow replied before getting up and walking towards her room.

Chris followed her. He was so close behind her that she could feel his breath on the nape of her neck as she opened the door to the bedroom. His breath sent chills down her spine, but she knew she had to remain calm. She refused to let Chris know that he had the upper hand.

Once in the room, Tomorrow grabbed one of her bags and pulled out her favorite oversized Bob Marley T-shirt. She usually slept naked, but she didn't need to give Chris any reason to make a move.

She slowly undressed as Chris' eyes remained glued to her curves. She pulled the T-shirt over her locs and onto her voluptuous frame.

"Mmm," Chris moaned and shook his head.

"What?"

"Nothing."

"Why are you shaking your head then?" Tomorrow questioned.

"I was just admiring you. Shawty, you got it," Chris said before he plopped down on the bed.

Instead of giving a seductive reply, Tomorrow flashed a smile and brushed her long locs off her shoulders.

Chris began to undress as well. He took off his shirt, revealing the body of a god. His chocolate skin glistened like it had been kissed by the midnight skies.

Next, he took off his jeans, revealing a nice sized notch in his boxers. Tomorrow looked away. A puddle started to form in her panties and a tingling sensation rushed through her. She knew that if she didn't get a grip, she was going to be bent over the bed before the night was over, and he might end up dead.

She frantically ran to her duffel bag and retrieved her blue pill box.

"Wednesday, Wednesday, Wednesday. There it is," Tomorrow said to herself before lifting the cap labeled "W" and removing three pills.

She quickly popped them and walked back over to the bed.

She hoped that Chris wouldn't ask her about them. He looked at her for a second to make sure everything was cool.

"You good, shawty?"

"Yeah, just had to take my BC."

"Is that right?" Chris enticingly asked.

"Knock it off," Tomorrow joked.

Without another word, Chris pulled back the covers and got into bed. He lay on his back and looked up at the ceiling. After turning off the lights, Tomorrow snuggled underneath the covers and made sure that she was comfortable. She felt her body relax and knew that sleep wasn't too far away.

The silence was unsettling. Chris wanted to know more about Tomorrow and figured that the only way to truly break the ice would be through a real conversation.

"Can I ask you a question?" Chris asked, breaking the silence.

Tomorrow turned and faced Chris. She wasn't sure of what he wanted to ask, but she was curious to know what was on his mind.

"What are you afraid of?" he asked.

"Excuse me?"

"You heard me. What are you afraid of?"

Chris sat up in the bed with his back to the bed's head board and turned on the lights. He at Tomorrow with a serious look on his face.

"Who said I was afraid?" Tomorrow snapped.

She sat up and crossed her legs. What was Chris trying to insinuate?

"What are you afraid of?" he repeated.

"Nothing," Tomorrow said with an attitude.

"We all afraid of something, Tomorrow. So, what are you afraid of?"

Tomorrow didn't like being vulnerable. She felt like there was a possibility that she could eventually learn to trust Chris, but allowing him to see her emotional side so soon just wasn't an option. She wasn't ready to relinquish that kind of control, especially not to a man. Besides, she learned from her past that being too vulnerable could lead you into a world of trouble.

But Chris was different; she knew in her heart that he wouldn't judge her for her past, the very past that she shielded from everyone. It just wasn't the right time, and oddly enough, the right time just never seemed to come.

"Failure," Tomorrow replied. "I'm afraid that if I'm not perfect, I will fail and to me, that's the worst thing that could ever happen."

"Is that why you walk around with this 'little miss perfect' image?" Chris inquired.

"It's a long story." Tomorrow sighed.

"I'm listening," Chris responded.

Chris knew that Tomorrow wasn't everything she appeared to be, but that's what intrigued him about her. The fact that she had everyone partially fooled showed that her mind was on a totally different level from most. He wasn't sure of the specifics, but he knew there was more to her than just what she revealed on the outside. He wanted to know the true Tomorrow.

"My mother is a perfectionist. She raised me the same way. Everything has to be damn near perfect and failure is not an option. Oh, and everything must be done a certain way for the betterment of her fucking plan."

"Wow. So what's the plan?"

"You know what? 'Til this day, I'm still not really sure. Who the fuck really knows what my mom wants? All I know is that she wants to build an empire of perfection, even down to who I'm dating. She'd have a fit if she knew I was dating anything less than a church boy or a senator's kid."

"So you're basically trapped inside this person that yo' moms wants you to be, but the real Tomorrow occasionally slips out from time to time?" Chris asked, attempting to rationalize what he just heard.

"Honestly, I don't know who the fuck I am sometimes. I kinda just go with the flow and what feels good at the moment because trying to rationalize this shit hurts my fucking head. I just know that I've always been who she wanted me to be, even when the shit didn't work out in my favor. I'm stuck. Stuck in between who I pretend to be, who I am, and who I've always wanted to be."

"So who do you want to be?"

"I just wanna be me."

"Do that then. What's the issue?" Chris didn't quite understand. Tomorrow was dealing with some inner demons that made it difficult for that answer to be so cut and dry.

"Once I figure that shit out, I'll let you know," Tomorrow joked. "But enough about me." She gently put her hand on Chris' leg. "What are you afraid of?"

Chris looked down at Tomorrow's hand on his leg. Even her slight touch sent chills through him. He wondered if he had that same effect on her.

"Love," he hesitantly replied.

"Love? What do you mean you're afraid of love? I've known you for over a year now and I've seen you with plenty

121

ho—females."

Chris laughed when he caught Tomorrow's Freudian slip.

"Exactly, but how long did they stick around?"

"Not long at all." Tomorrow laughed.

"That's why. I purposely talk to females who I know ain't really on my level mentally. It's easier to just fuck a bad ass chick and keep it moving. Nice and clean. Everybody gets what they want out of the deal and nobody gets hurt," Chris explained.

"Sound kinda shallow don't you think?"

"Probably, but I'm sure you can relate."

Yep, Tomorrow thought to herself. She definitely could relate. She never kept a dude around long enough to fall for him. She satisfied her sexual urges and then she moved on to the next. She had suffered enough heartache and pain over the years, so to her, men were nothing more than walking dildos and simple manipulation tools.

"Mos' def. But I wouldn't say I was afraid," Tomorrow admitted.

"So what would you call it?"

"Cautious."

Chris laughed.

"What's so funny?" Tomorrow asked.

"You are. See, that's the difference between you and me, I'm not in denial about my shit. Once you stop trying to live in a fantasy world, all that inner shit you got going on will be much easier to deal with." Chris broke it down.

He was right. Tomorrow spent way too much time trying to shield everything. When was she going to just let it all out and finally allow herself to be free?

"Oh really?"

"Yes really. Listen, Tomorrow, you and me, we two of

a kind. I know that shit. I can feel it. Two peas in a fucking pod, but see, I've learned to elevate above all the bullshit and you still floating around in it. Let it go."

"So if you let all that shit go, then why are you still fucking around with random chicks, huh Dr. Phil?" Tomorrow joked.

"I don't know. Maybe I'm waiting on you."

There was an awkward silence between the two.

Chris leaned over and gently kissed Tomorrow. Once he tasted the sweetness of her lips, he didn't want to stop. Chris softly caressed her face and continued to place his gentle kisses on her warm and juicy lips. His pulse began racing at warped speed and he immediately became erect, something he had never experienced before, at least not in the same way, and it made him nervous. He quickly broke the kiss. Tomorrow sat quietly and just stared at him with a look that he really couldn't read.

"My bad. I was just in the moment. You know how that shit goes," Chris joked to lighten the mood.

There was intense sexual tension and they both felt it. Neither one of them wanted to make the first move, but that kiss had ignited something between them that they simply couldn't deny. Taking it any further at this point wasn't an option, and out of fear, they both held back.

"It's koo. It was nice," Tomorrow softly responded.

"True," Chris said.

"Well, I enjoyed the talk. Thanks for being open with me," he continued.

"Anytime. I like talking to you. I feel like I can tell you anything."

Tomorrow rested on the bed and got comfortable. After turning off the lights, Chris laid down too.

He moved in closer to Tomorrow and wrapped his arm

around her. He wanted to be close. The magnetic force between them, ignited from the kiss, had him yearning to experience that feeling again.

Generally, cuddling was a no go for Tomorrow, but this was different. It felt natural and real to her, and she silently wished she could stay in that moment forever. It was almost as if it were a dream. But unfortunately, she knew that dreams never ended very well in her world.

"Goodnight," Chris whispered to her.

"Goodnight."

***

Kane tossed and turned as he lay next to Legacy. He just couldn't get comfortable. He wanted to have sex, but he didn't want to do it with Legacy. Knowing that Tomorrow's sweet pussy was less than a few feet away and he couldn't get a taste of it had him livid.

To be honest, he was still pissed off over the lack of attention that Tomorrow had shown him. She had barely uttered two words to him since he walked in the door, and yet, she had become so comfy with Chris. To add insult to injury, he knew that Tomorrow and Chris were sharing a room, and that pissed him off even more.

Just thinking about Tomorrow caused his dick to get hard. He imagined her walking into the den and straddling his dick like a pro. But instead, he looked over and saw Legacy, a disappointment in his mind. He watched her sleep for a few moments and contemplated whether or not he should get in a quickie.

"Yo Legacy, wake up," Kane whispered.

He pushed her over on her back, but Legacy didn't respond. Kane slipped his hand under her shirt to cop a feel, and she immediately became irritated.

"So you ain't kicking it with your boo tonight?" she questioned.

Legacy turned over and faced Kane so that he could see the look of disgust written across her face.

"I already told you that I ain't fuck Mishon! Damn, you stay on that bullshit! Now can we fuck or what? Before a nigga catch blue balls and shit!"

Little did Kane know, Legacy wasn't referring to Mishon. She knew the truth about him creeping with Tomorrow, but instead of just coming clean, she wanted to string everybody along just like they had done her.

"Nigga, make it quick!"

She took her panties off and flung them across the room. She rolled over to the side and lifted up her leg up, nonverbally giving Kane an invitation to start.

Kane was too drunk to even argue. He slid on his condom and penetrated her with no regard. His strokes lacked passion. He simply wanted to bust a nut and go to bed.

"Ouch, Kane that hurt," Legacy complained.

"Well, go get the baby oil."

"So you don't eat pussy no more? Or maybe you just eat her pussy!"

"Look Legacy, can you please shut the fuck up? Here, just bend over so we can really get this shit over with," Kane slurred.

Kane roughly flipped Legacy over on her knees and sexed her doggy style. He thought about Tomorrow the entire time, but it just didn't feel the same.

Right about now, Tomorrow would be throwing her ass back and reaching underneath to play with his balls as he stroked her pussy. But Legacy, no, she didn't know anything about that. She was an amateur in the sex department, and Kane was way overdue for an upgrade.

When Legacy tried to flip back over, Kane grabbed hold of her shoulders and dug deeper to keep her in place. There was a reason Kane had her bent over: he didn't want to see her face.

It all lasted about a half an hour, but twenty minutes of it was nothing but Legacy's complaining.

Once Kane had his release, without any words, he pulled up his shorts and walked over to his twin bed.

"Oh, so now you just going to take my pussy and run!" Legacy screamed.

Kane ignored her. He took off his clothes and passed out on the bed, leaving Legacy awake to nag herself.

"I know you hear me, Kane! That's right, act like you don't give a damn about me, but I'm carrying your baby, nigga! Once I give birth, I'mma take your ass straight to the courthouse, cuz you gonna be on them papers for the next eighteen years, nigga!"

Before, long the only sounds she could hear were those of Kane snoring. Fortunately for him, he was pissy drunk, because had he been sober, he probably wouldn't have gotten any rest.

Legacy was too hyper to go back to sleep. She needed to confirm what Kane's mother accidentally revealed. She picked his shorts up off the floor and pulled his cell phone out of the pocket.

Like a pro, Legacy turned Kane's phone on vibrate so that he wouldn't catch her snooping.

"Time to check your pictures and your text messages." She laughed.

Shockingly, Legacy found nothing that would link him to Tomorrow, but she still wasn't convinced that they hadn't hooked up on the sneak tip.

Legacy was disappointed. She was sure that looking

126

through Kane's phone would reveal everything that she needed to know. Feeling defeated, she tiptoed back to his pants and placed the phone where she found in.

She jumped and almost fell over when she thought she had been caught, but quickly noticed that Kane was still fast asleep. He was making strange noises and uttering words in his sleep. Legacy's panic turned to anger when she realized that Kane was having a sex dream, one that she knew had nothing to do with her.

"You nasty bitch you," he moaned.

Legacy got back in bed and enjoyed the show.

"I got you," she threatened.

CHAPTER

~ 13 ~

It was the middle of a Saturday afternoon, and Mishon was just waking up. She got herself together and decided to plan out her day. She figured that she would go shopping and hoped that she wouldn't have to go alone. Brandon wasn't feeling well, so he decided to stay in bed for the rest of the day.

"Here, take this money and pick me up some Pepto-Bismol or something."

"Ain't nobody else up. Who's gonna go shopping with me?"

Mishon poked out her bottom lip and tried her best to give Brandon a sad face.

"Oh, hell nah! You better wake Tomorrow's ass up and see if she will ride."

"But her and Chris are still knocked out."

"Well, I don't know what to tell you."

Mishon climbed back into the bed. She kissed and tickled Brandon, hoping it would persuade him to accompany her.

They both heard a noise in the kitchen. It sounded like someone opening the refrigerator door and it stopped Mishon and Brandon in their tracks.

"See, that might be her in the kitchen," Brandon predicted.

"Go see."

Brandon playfully shoved Mishon, attempting to push her out of the bed and onto the floor.

"Fuck you, Brandon," she jokingly replied.

"We just finished that about three hours ago."

Mishon jumped to her feet, walked out the bedroom and entered the kitchen to see who was making all of the commotion. There she found Legacy leaning over the counter taking her asthma medication and wheezing like a fat kid at weight camp.

Mishon turned her back immediately and hoped that Legacy wouldn't see her.

I definitely ain't going with that dusty bitch, she thought as she walked towards the living room.

Legacy noticed Mishon and thought that it was the perfect chance to tell Mishon everything that she had discovered about Tomorrow. She followed her into the living room.

"Mishon, can I talk to you? I found some things out that you should really know."

"No, you cannot."

"Ah, come on girl, we been friends for years."

"I can't tell by the way you tried to jump on me at Trell's party."

"I thought we squashed this shit yesterday?"

"We did, but I ain't forgot, bitch! You still on my shit list."

"Shon, c'mon, I said I was sorry."

"Fine, what do you need to talk to me about, chick?"

"How about we take a walk on the beach where we can really be alone."

Mishon didn't want to be anywhere near Legacy, but she couldn't fight the urge; she was always a sucker for juicy gossip.

The beach was only a few steps away from the condo. Once they reached the sand, they found a nice spot to set up their beach chairs.

"This better be good, cuz I was supposed to go shopping," Mishon said in an uninterested tone.

"I went to Kane's house a while back and his mother let me know that some chick with a black BMW was creepin' over there late at night," Legacy began.

"Okay, is that it?"

"And even at Trell's party, I caught Kane and Tomorrow looking at each other in a funny way," she continued. "I think they're fucking."

Mishon was hearing old news. That whole affair had been going on for at least a year, and frankly, she was tired of hearing about it.

"Well, you going to have to talk to Tomorrow about that, cuz I have no clue what's going on. Kane is a super ho, so he could be sleeping with any and everything," Mishon stated.

Legacy was thrown off by Mishon's nonchalant attitude. Mishon was supposed to be her best friend, so why wasn't she more concerned? They were supposed to be way closer than Mishon could ever be with Tomorrow, but that seemed to no longer be the case.

"Well, that's not all. I found out that Tomorrow was taking medication for bipolar type II and—"

"Wait! How did you find that out?" Mishon interrupted.

She sat up in her beach chair and peered at Legacy with a curious yet skeptical stare. Mishon wasn't sure how Legacy had come about this information, but she knew that it wasn't done legitimately.

"Well, I saw her prescription bottle in her purse. I took it out and researched the medication," Legacy lied.

"You went in her purse?"

"I mean, I was curious."

"You went in her purse?" Mishon repeated and shook her head in disgust.

"This bitch is on all kinds of shit, from Lithium to—"

"Stop it! I don't want to hear anymore. If you stay outta other people's business, then you would have no choice but to tend to your own."

"But—"

"Nah, this conversation is over. That's so fucked up."

Mishon got up and paced back to the house thinking about what she had just heard. She never saw Tomorrow take medication for anything.

It was very possible that Legacy had truly discovered this information, but it was even more possible that Legacy was just being Legacy, a girl who thrived off of starting unnecessary drama. Either way, she wasn't going get in the middle of it, at least not yet.

Legacy stayed behind at the beach and wondered what had just happened. It seemed as if Mishon was defending Tomorrow instead of taking her findings seriously. She was still taken aback by the fact that Mishon didn't even flinch when she told her that Tomorrow was really the one sleeping with Kane. That made Legacy suspicious. She had a feeling that Mishon knew more than she would admit, but Legacy simply didn't have the proof.

"Brandon, get up!"

Mishon busted through the door of the condo's master bedroom in a rage.

"Dammit, Mishon, I told you I ain't fucking around today. Did you get my Pepto-Bismol?"

"Nah, I ain't go to the store yet. Legacy asked to speak to me in private, so we ended up going to the beach."

"Oh, so now that chick wanna talk after she tried to show off at Trell n'em party."

"Umm-hmm, but Brandon, I need you to really listen to what I was told."

Mishon sat down on the bed and stared at Brandon. He knew that what she had to say must be serious because she refused to just let it rest.

"Well, can a nigga at least get some water and aspirin? Shit, I told you I don't feel good! I shouldn't have drunk that whole bottle of VSOP last night. I shoulda just stuck to my few blunts and that's it. Fucking with y'all alcoholics. I know that nigga Chris gotta be still fucked up too."

Mishon raced to the kitchen to get Brandon some water. She went into their bathroom and got three Tylenol Extra Strength pills and rushed back to him. She hoped that the pills would do the trick so he could stop his whining and finally listen to what she had to say.

"Here, Brandon, now can you shut the hell up and listen?" Mishon asked in an annoyed tone.

Brandon slowly placed all three pills in his mouth and

chased them down with some water. After swallowing, he playfully smacked his lips.

"Ahhhh. That's some good ass water, Shon."

"Brandon, I'm fucking serious, nigga!"

"Okay, damn, what's good?"

"Legacy told me that Kane's mother told her she been seeing a black BMW coming by on the late night."

"Hold up, they still been creepin' since the party? I thought you told me that she been carried that nigga?"

"Yeah, she did, but obviously now, Legacy knows it wasn't me. I ain't got no Beamer. Plus, that ho went in Tomorrow's purse and found all types of medication for bipolar disorder," Mishon explained.

"And, so what?" Brandon said calmly. "Baby, you would be surprised what muthafuckas have in their medicine cabinet. I bet that bitch Legacy is on something too. Shit, cuz she surely act like it. That bitch be on some ova shit."

"True dat," Mishon agreed.

"And as far as that Kane shit is concerned, so the fuck what? That was never your business to begin with, so just stay the fuck outta it before you get that nigga split in two." Brandon scowled at Mishon.

"Now look, I know that you and Legacy were cool, but don't let her fill your head up with all this nonsense. Even if it's true about your girl, Tomorrow ain't never did nothing to make you not trust her, so nothing should change. Besides, Legacy so worried about what Kane up to, that she's trying to get you sucked into all that drama, and I ain't having it. I need you to be worried about us and what we got going on. Fuck allat other shit."

"You're right."

Mishon felt a lot better after talking to Brandon. He made some very valid points about the entire situation. She figured it was best to just stay out of it and let Tomorrow deal with the accusations. But one thing was for sure, Mishon was definitely going to let Tomorrow know about what Kane's mother had revealed.

"Hey babe," Brandon spoke again, "but what about that Pepto-Bismol?"

CHAPTER

~ 14 ~

Tomorrow and Chris finally woke from their drug induced state. Chris left the room to go find Brandon so that they could enjoy their "breakfast blunt."

Tomorrow wanted to see what Mishon was up to for the day. She poked her head out of her bedroom and saw her standing right in front of the door.

"Good Morning." Tomorrow grinned.

"No, ho, you mean good afternoon." Mishon giggled.

"All the same during a vacation. What you got going on for today?"

"Well, I was supposed to go shopping this morning, but

Legacy informed me of something that I think you should know."

Tomorrow walked back into the room and prepared for her shower. She could care less about what Legacy had to say.

"What'd that bitch say now?"

"Tomorrow she told me that Kane's mother told her about you coming to see Kane on the late night. Talkin' about seeing your black BMW coming through all the time."

"Oh well, me and Kane have been done for a while now. That bitch don't want it with me for real! As you can see, she ain't said nothing to me yet about it. Why wait? If somebody was fucking my man, I would've been addressed the situation!" Tomorrow felt her blood boil.

"True but it seems like she's trying to figure you out or something."

"Figure me out? Fuck that fake fetus having, dick riding trick! I ain't with that shit! Matter fact, where that ho at? I will tell her myself that I fucked her man! I will fuck her man again and make that bitch watch! I should do that shit too," Tomorrow said in a fit of rage.

"Whoa! Tomorrow, chill out!" Mishon interrupted. "Girl, you okay? I ain't never seen you like this before."

Tomorrow took a few moments to calm down. She was shocked that she had flipped out that way, especially in front of Mishon.

"Girl, my bad for that episode, I can get a bit cranky when I'm tired. I'mma go take a shower. Don't go nowhere, cuz I want to talk to you went I get out. That bitch Legacy is really trying me now!"

Tomorrow was embarrassed that she had just had such an episode in front of Mishon.

Her moods were becoming more frequent and erratic, but with her meds, Tomorrow could usually keep it cool, calm, and collected. Lately, however, it seemed like she just couldn't stay in control of her emotions.

Because of the killing, her psychosis had arrived at a whole new level, and she was afraid that she wouldn't be able to come back from it.

Tomorrow grabbed her bag full of toiletries and went into the bathroom. She immediately took out her pillbox and swallowed three pills. She paced back and forth from one end of the bathroom to the other.

"Lord, give me strength before I rip out that bitch's uterus and drive over it with my car," she prayed.

Tomorrow felt an overwhelming urge to scream, but fought against the desire. She knew that Mishon was just a few steps away and would really think something was up.

She dropped to her knees and quietly sobbed. Holding in her secret, all of her secrets, had become unbearable. She was tired of pretending to be somebody that she wasn't, someone who she really didn't know.

"Deep breaths, deep breaths. Tomorrow, get it together," she whispered to herself.

She grabbed a handful of her locs with both hands and pulled them until the pain became real.

"Bitch, you've been in there for five minutes and I don't hear no water running in that muthafucka. Are you aight in there?" Mishon screamed outside of the bathroom door.

Hearing Mishon's voice snapped Tomorrow out of her trance. She hurriedly stood to her feet and straightened out her locs.

"I'm fine, girl. That Cuervo got me messed up. I suggest you back up a lil' bit before you get a good whiff of this shit," Tomorrow lied.

"Yo' ole stanky booty ass." Mishon laughed as she walked back over towards the bed.

Tomorrow undressed and turned on the shower. Once she got in, she felt much better. The hot water poured over her body and she felt the ultimate release. Although the medication hadn't completely kicked in, she felt like she was finally releasing some of her stress.

Mishon patiently waited on the bed. She couldn't help but notice Tomorrow's cell phone vibrating uncontrollably. She walked over to the dresser and picked it up.

Shock immediately spread across her face when she looked down and saw a lot of threatening messages coming through.

Bitch this shit aint over. Imma fuckin kill you when I catch up with U.

What the fuck, who is this talkin' 'bout ripping her a new asshole? she thought.

"Don't worry bitch Imma fuck your dead body and after that imma stick my dick so far down your throat that you burp my semen!" Mishon read aloud.

Mishon couldn't read anymore. She knew that it was officially time to ask Tomorrow what was really going on. It was clear that she had some serious issues that needed to be addressed.

When Tomorrow came back into the room to get dressed, she seemed more calm and ready to talk. She went to the closet and pulled out her favorite maxi dress.

"Girl, what you think about this little number I bought from Saks Fifth Ave?"

"Look, Tomorrow, I don't give a fuck about that dress right now. I looked at your phone because it was vibrating off the hook while you were in the shower."

"And?"

Tomorrow picked up her phone and saw a slew of nasty messages. She knew that it was time to talk and get everything off her chest.

"Umm hmm, now who the fuck is that threatening to shoot you in the pussy?" Mishon asked.

"Quan," she muttered while lotioning her body.

"Nigga from the party?" Mishon was confused.

"Yes."

"So, why the fuck is he threatening you? What happened?"

"Bitch, it's a long story. Promise me you won't judge me when I tell you what the fuck happened?"

Mishon got nervous. She knew it had to be serious if Tomorrow was making her promise something like that.

"What the fuck, Tomorrow? Spill it!"

"Not until you promise me."

"Okay. I promise."

***

Quan grabbed Tomorrow by the hand and led her up to the entrance of his apartment building. Tomorrow observed her surroundings closely. Although Quan seemed harmless, she made sure she that she knew her location just in case he started tripping.

She saw a sign that read Carver Hill Apartments, and that's when she realized they were in one of the worst hoods in Southeast D.C. She was in the middle of Barry Farm.

Tomorrow wasn't afraid, she had been in worst situations, but what bothered her was the fact that there was no way that Quan had a luxury apartment.

Several stray cats ran out as Quan and Tomorrow walked into the building. That was another indication that Quan's appearance didn't truly reveal his financial status. She tried to keep an open mind.

She followed Quan to his door and waited as he unlocked it. After Quan opened the door, he stepped to the side so that Tomorrow could view his apartment.

He smiled.

"Well. This is my spot. Come on in," Quan said.

An unidentifiable nervous feeling swept over Tomorrow, and she immediately wanted to run in the other direction.

I'm too damn shallow for my own good, she thought as she forced herself to walk over the threshold.

The smell of destruction and dog piss instantly filled Tomorrow's nose and she wanted to vomit. She was located in what looked to be a living room, only there was no couch. A small floral love seat for two sat in the middle of the empty space. The love seat didn't look safe for sitting. The cushion was so damaged that the springs were visible. His beige carpet had a crusted brown tint and it was clear that it had been around for a long time.

Everything from old chewing gum, to cigarette burns, and even Kool-Aid stains, dwelled on the rug.

Ughh, Tomorrow thought to herself.

She was disgusted at how bad Quan kept his place. She just couldn't understand why he would ever bring a female to a place that looked so awful.

"Make yourself at home. You want something to drink?" Quan asked.

"Nigga, no," Tomorrow blurted without thinking.

How could she have gotten herself into this mess? Quan was fine as hell, but definitely wasn't fine enough for her to ruin her pink Sergio Rossi Laser Cut Sandals over.

"Excuse the mess. I've been meaning to get this shit together. You good?" Quan laughed as he reached for her hand.

"No. I'm not good. Is that a dog over there in that cage?" Tomorrow yanked her hand back.

When she noticed the frail pet humped over in his cage,

she was officially done.

The dog's color matched the dingy carpet. He was so thin that you could clearly see his ribs. He had dark bags under his eyes, patches in his fur, and he looked as if he didn't have much time left on earth. The dog's cage was filled with its own feces, and Tomorrow was surprised that the dog was even still alive.

That must be where the awful stench is coming from.

"Yeah. That's Bruno, he over there chillin' right now."

"That don't look like chillin', that's death. He looks hungry, nigga, when the last time you fed him?" Tomorrow said in a disgusted tone.

"I fed him before I left for the party. I've had Bruno for years now."

"You need to take him to the vet, he looks sick. As a matter of fact, guessing from the smell that's coming from him, he ain't gonna make it much longer. We should just take him out back and shoot him. Hopefully, the saying is true and all dogs really do go to heaven." Tomorrow laughed.

"Bitch, ain't nobody shooting my dog!" Quan boldly replied.

He was offended.

"I'm just saying, nigga, like we can go right out back and I'll do that nigga in for you. No charge."

"Aye, stop talking 'bout my muthafucking dog, bitch, I ain't playing!"

"You're right. I'm just gonna go. I can't take this. These are very expensive shoes, and I don't think they go well with vomit and dog piss."

Tomorrow walked towards the door to exit, but Quan stopped her from leaving. He didn't understand why Tomorrow was being so bougie. He hated females who thought they were too good to have a good time. He knew that she didn't like his place from the moment she walked in, but he felt that she could've at least pretended things were good, especially when he went out of his way to be so hospitable.

Before Tomorrow could leave, Quan hit her over the head with his bare fist and watched her fall to the floor. He was going to teach her some damn respect.

Tomorrow awoke to the smell of weed and piss. Her head was pounding and her vision was still a bit blurred. It took her a moment to realize where she was. She was still at Quan's house, only now, she was tied to a wobbly chair in his bedroom.

She wondered how much time had gone by and if Quan had done anything crazy to her.

Fortunately, she didn't feel strange down below, so she knew he hadn't raped her. She looked around and noticed that she was in his room. Although it was cleaner than the rest of the apartment, it still made her cringe.

Across the room, she noticed that there was a video camera set up with a red light blinking on the side. It was recording every moment that went on in the room, and Tomorrow knew that once she escaped, she'd have to destroy it immediately.

She looked over and noticed that Quan was sitting on a single mattress on the floor, playing video games. The mattress was bare. There were no fitted sheets, only a balled up comforter that didn't appear to have a high quality thread count.

She wondered why anyone would sleep on a mattress with no sheets. When she looked up at his bedroom window, she knew why. Quan had turned his batman bed sheets into curtains.

Sheets are made for beds, and this nigga got them up as curtains. How clever.

She couldn't help but giggle to herself at the thought.

When Quan heard Tomorrow's laughter, he looked over at her.

"Oh, you woke," he said nonchalantly.

"You thirsty, gotta go to the bathroom or something? You been out for a while now."

"Nigga, you got sheets for curtains and a rotting dog in the living room. You honestly think that I'm gonna use your bathroom?" Tomorrow mocked.

"Bitch, I told you stop talking 'bout my dog!" Quan yelled.

"Nigga, quit bitching. Let me go! Why the fuck do you have me tied up anyway?"

"Because you're very disrespectful. You VA bitches are all the same. You play with a nigga's emotions, and then when it's time to give it up, you wanna act brand new. So I said fuck it, lemme tie this bitch up."

Quan had a calm look on his face. He didn't seem crazy, but his words just didn't sit right with Tomorrow. She knew what she had to do.

"Nigga, this entire house smells like dog piss. Do you really expect to get pussy in a place like this?" Tomorrow laughed.

"That's what I mean. You uppity VA bitches don't respect shit. I'mma real ass nigga, got my own place and take care of my shit. What the fuck was you expecting, a mansion?"

"Negro, do you see these shoes? These shoes probably cost more than your entire rent. Did you really think you were gonna bring me in this death trap and fuck my brains out? This is expensive pussy."

"Well, I'll tell you what. If I don't get none of that expensive pussy you got, bitch you ain't leaving!"

"You are fucking crazy! What are you gonna do, rape me?" Tomorrow became a bit distraught. She was almost due for another dose of her meds, and if she didn't get them soon, she was liable to go postal.

"Rape? Nah, bitch, you crazy. I don't get down like that. You gon' give it to me and I'mma tape that shit!"

Quan was obviously delusional. Although Tomorrow found him a bit amusing, she really didn't have time for this drama. Had she known that Quan was a maniac, she would've called up Kane for one last fuck session instead.

"Well, that ain't gonna happen, dude. You better let me go."

"Or what?" Quan mocked.

"Or I'mma kill your punk ass. Matter of fact, I'mma slice you from ear to fucking ear, bitch," Tomorrow threatened.

"Bitch, you tied up. How u gonna do that?"

"You better just keep your eyes open, cuz once I get loose, it's a wrap."

"Whatever. You thirtsty?" Quan said, changing the subject.

"Nigga, let me go!" Tomorrow screamed.

"Aint no use yelling, bitch, I live alone and this is the fucking hood, section 8, bitch. Ain't nobody coming to the rescue. What *Tony! Toni! Tone! say?* It's just me and yoooou!" Quan sang off key.

Tomorrow became more aggravated by the second. The wobbly chair she sat in only fueled the fire. Every time she moved, the chair leaned to the other side, unevenly flopping from side to side.

Flip flop flip flop flip flop

"AHHHHHH!" Tomorrow screamed.

"Bitch, what's the problem now?" Quan responded.

"Nigga, you couldn't have found a chair with all four legs in working fucking condition?!"

Quan just stared at her. He couldn't believe that she was complaining about a chair when she was tied up. He had no intensions of actually hurting Tomorrow; he just wanted to scare her. He had met plenty of bougie chicks, but he thought that Tomorrow would be different. He wanted to teach her a lesson and prove that she wasn't any better than the chicks that he normally brought back to the house and had sex with.

"You can't be serious. You tied up, bitch, and all you can do is complain about a broken chair?"

Quan found it quite odd that Tomorrow wasn't frightened.

She's just trying to play hard, he thought to himself.

He decided that he'd keep up with the charade as long as he could. He knew that eventually, she'd just give it up and he'd be able to throw it in her face that she gave her "expensive ass pussy" to a "broke ass nigga" like him.

After a few hours, Quan realized that he wasn't dealing with an amateur. Tomorrow stared at him with a look that could kill and wouldn't blink. He found himself getting nervous and not sure of the next step to take. He honestly thought that he'd be deep in the pussy by now and laughing with his boys about how he banged some bougie Virginia chick.

Unfortunately, Tomorrow was resilient and wouldn't be giving up that easily. Quan knew that he had gone too far, but it was too late to turn back now. If Tomorrow wouldn't give in, he'd just keep her there until she finally did.

All night, Quan looked over at Tomorrow and wondered how long she would take to give in. He was almost too nervous to go to sleep. He tried his best to stay awake but knew that eventually he would pass out. Although he knew there was no way she could escape, Quan couldn't help but imagine him waking up and finding her standing over him with a butcher knife. He literally slept with one eye open all night.

The next day, Quan went on with his daily activities as usual and acted as if nothing was wrong with having someone tied up in his bedroom. He played video games, sent text messages, and even masturbated as if Tomorrow was not in the room.

"You hungry?" Quan broke the silence.

He bit into his fried bologna sandwich and then held it out as a peace offering.

"I don't eat bologna," Tomorrow said flatly.

"You real rude, bitch. I'm trying my best to be a good host, but you making it difficult. Are you always so fucking up-tight?" Quan laughed.

"Only when I'm being kidnapped by dumb ass niggas with raggedy ass apartments."

"Whoa, kidnapped? Bitch, I ain't kidnap you. You came to my house willingly!" Quan defended himself.

"Man, I swear the ammonia from that dog piss must got you losing brain cells, cuz nigga, you's an idiot." Tomorrow shook her head and laughed.

"Bitch, fuck the small talk. You ready for some of this dick yet?"

"This is your brain on drugs, nigga." Tomorrow continued laughing.

There was no way that Quan was that dumb. How had she missed it? Not to mention that after seeing him in the light and through sober eyes, she realized that he wasn't as fine as he appeared to be in the dark.

Tomorrow pitied Quan, not because of his living environment, but because he had no idea of the things that she was capable of, and as soon as she had the chance, she would kill him without a second thought.

"Don't you have work to do or something? You've been here all morning." Tomorrow was irritated and tired of seeing Quan's face.

"Nope, I ain't got no job. I lost my gig two months ago,

so I've been filing unemployment."

"Figures."

"Bitch, you wasn't saying that shit when you was grinding all up on a nigga. You VA bitches…"

"Nigga, save it," Tomorrow interrupted. "Don't say nothing else about VA bitches when you got a muthafuckin' sheet hanging up on that window. I bet you use one as a shower curtain too, huh?" Tomorrow laughed.

Quan paused before responding. He did have a sheet as a shower curtain.

"Fuck you, ho."

"Nigga, you wish. This whole apartment smells like dog piss, fart, and death. You have the nerve to even talk about uppity bitches. Any bitch that you had up in here willingly probably needs a tetanus shot. That or some penicillin."

"Bitch, I'm warning you," Quan said angrily.

"Instead of kidnapping pussy, you need to be taking Fido out to the back and filling that nigga with bullets. PETA would have a fuckin' fit if they knew you had that damn dog in that cage like that. Nigga look like he ain't had a meal in years."

Quan walked over to Tomorrow and backhanded her in the face. It felt good for him to release his anger. She had been mocking him for the last two nights and he was tired of her smart mouth.

Tomorrow's head flung from one side to the other. She felt a spot of blood trickle from her lips.

"That's all you got?" She laughed. "Nigga, you're so wack. Matter of fact, once I kill you, I might just put lil' ole Rosco out his misery too. Two to the head, nigga, two to the—" Tomorrow couldn't finish her statement.

Quan kicked her so hard in the stomach that she flew back in the chair and hit the floor. The force from the kick caused Tomorrow to vomit.

"Now, I told you to stop talking 'bout my fucking dog, bitch. I'm not taking no more shit from you!"

Quan exited the room in a rage. After about twenty minutes, he came back with some Hot Pockets and a Sprite. He looked down at Tomorrow with a guilty expression on his face.

His look read that he felt bad about hurting her. He sat the chair back on its feet and wiped the side of her face with a dirty Wu Tang T-shirt.

"You wan' a bite of this?" he asked, holding the hot pocket up to her face.

"No," Tomorrow nonchalantly responded and turned away.

"You ain't really ate nothing yet. I know you gotta be hungry."

"I'd rather starve."

"If we just fuck and get it over with, you can go. I know you gonna like it. My dick is huge," Quan joked.

"So is your brother's. What's your point?"

"Fine, bitch. Sit here and don't eat then. I don't give a fuck anymore." Quan gave up.

Hours passed and Tomorrow was getting woozy. She was hungry, dehydrated and had a thirst to do some bodily harm. Without her meds, she was definitely in rare form. All she needed was one chance to escape, and Quan was going to wish he had never crossed her.

Quan left to go to the store and Tomorrow was all alone in the room, left with her own sinister thoughts. She quickly conjured her plan of escape. She knew that it would probably involve her giving up some pussy.

Tomorrow decided she'd give Quan exactly what he wanted, but what he didn't know was that it would come with the ultimate price.

When he returned, Tomorrow put on her best charm. She knew that Quan would be putty in her hands once she convinced him that she wanted him. Besides, it had been days since she had sex. She would enjoy this as much as he would.

Quan sat on the lonely mattress and didn't even acknowledge Tomorrow. He played his video games and slurped on his Big Gulp. She knew that although he was mad, all she had to do was say she was ready and he would drop everything.

"You didn't bring me anything back from 7-11?" Tomorrow sparked conversation.

Quan jumped.

"Damn, I forgot you was here. You was acting all snotty, I didn't even think you knew what a 7-11 was," he joked.

Quan put the drink to his mouth and took the biggest gulp he could. He thought he was taunting Tomorrow, but little did he know, she was setting him up.

"I wonder if you slurp on pussy as good as you're doing that straw," Tomorrow said in a sensual voice.

Quan's eyes grew wide. He couldn't believe what he had just heard. He knew that it was just a matter of time before Tomorrow gave in, and that time had finally come.

He put his video game controller down next to him and looked in her direction.

"Don't say shit like that unless you're ready to get it in. I've been beating my dick all day thinking about how good that pussy probably is." Quan got excited.

"Oh, it's great. The best you'll ever have." Tomorrow laughed.

"So you want it?" Quan grabbed his dick.

"Only if it's good. I obviously don't need any more disappointments."

"You won't have to worry about that. My d game is on

point, shawty."

Quan walked over to Tomorrow's chair. He slid off her sandals and began to undress her from the waist down. He looked at her to make sure that she wasn't joking. Her eyes read that she was very serious, and that instantly made him hard.

"What are you doing?" She whispered.

"I'm not about to fuck you in this wobbly ass chair. Let me do this," Quan responded, acting as if he were a pro.

Once he slid off her panties, he admired her pussy. He put his arms underneath her thighs and lifted her towards him.

He immediately dove in and began sucking on Tomorrow's pussy as if he was on death row and she was his final meal.

Tomorrow didn't expect Quan to be so good. She found herself getting lost in the moment as he indulged in her wet juice box, but she knew she had to keep her eye on the prize. Quan had violated, and she had to let him know that it wouldn't be tolerated. Tomorrow would make an example out of him.

Quan flickered his tongue around Tomorrow's protruding clit and suckled it until he heard her gasp for air. He didn't mind that her pussy had been marinating for a few days. He was engulfed by the natural essence and wanted to feel his dick deep inside of her.

Lost in the moment himself, he hurriedly began to untie her.

"You won't run, will you?" Quan asked nervously.

"No. I'mma give you what you want," Tomorrow assured him.

When both hands were free, Quan picked Tomorrow up and continued eating her pussy all the way to the mattress on the floor. She couldn't deny it, Quan was definitely skilled with his tongue.

He slowly removed his dick from his boxers and smiled in delight. This was the moment that he had been waiting for.

Without warning, he shoved all eight inches deep inside of Tomorrow's pussy and almost fainted. He couldn't believe how tight and wet she was. He was so stuck that he couldn't even pump. He just lay inside of her for a few moments, hoping that the sensation to release would soon subside.

She pulled him close to her and whispered softly into his ears.

"You like that pussy don't you?"

"Hell yeah!" he moaned.

Quan closed his eyes and took a few quick pumps but quickly stopped when he felt the urge to nut again. He knew he would have to take it slow in order to make the moment truly last.

Tomorrow wrapped her arms around him and held him close. He went deeper inside her before letting out a huge scream, but it wasn't because he had just released. Tomorrow had slit him across the back of the neck with her razor blade.

"I told you I was gonna kill your punk ass, didn't I?" Tomorrow erotically whispered before Quan fell back.

"How the fuck?" He grabbed the back of his neck in agony.

"I don't wear a bun in my hair for no reason. You think I would go to a party and not have a lil' something on me? You a damn fool." Tomorrow laughed.

"Bitch!" Quan could barely move.

"And you had a nerve to go in me raw, nigga? Are you crazy? I'm really gonna fuck you up now!"

She kicked him in the balls and watched him squirm.

"You bitch!" Quan screamed in pain.

"Don't scream. Remember, it's just me and yoooou!"

Tomorrow mocked.

Blood trickled from his neck. This was Tomorrow's chance to finally escape, but she wasn't done with Quan just yet. She slit him again, but this time across the face. Seeing his blood sent her into a rage. Before she knew it, she had punched him so many times that her own fists were bloody red.

Dumb muthafucka. I can't even kill his dumb ass cuz he went up in me raw! Too much evidence!

The urge to finish the job was almost unbearable, but Tomorrow knew that her DNA would be easily traced if she killed him now. She would have to postpone murdering Quan until a later date.

He was a hood nigga, so she knew that there was no way he'd go to the police or even admit that he got hemmed up by some female. She knew that he'd be back and they would eventually have a fight to the death. His death.

"Just because you're not dead doesn't mean I'm not gonna kill you. I want you to suffer for a little bit." Tomorrow laughed before sealing his forehead with a kiss.

She wiped off the lipstick print with her hand. She wasn't done with him just yet, so she decided to save that kiss for later.

"I'll see you again, Quan. Thanks for the hospitality."

Tomorrow grabbed her clothes and slipped everything back on. She ran over to where Quan kept her purse and made sure that everything was still there. Sure enough, all of her money, cards, and even her phone were still in tact.

That dummy didn't even rob me? He musta been hard up for some pussy for real.

Before leaving, she decided to set poor Bruno free. Unfortunately, the dog was as dumb as his damn owner. He just sat there looking pitiful.

Oh well, I tried, she thought.

Tomorrow decided to make one more move before she left. She felt the urge to go to the bathroom. She had been holding it in for too long, but she knew that there was no way she would even step foot inside another part of Quan's apartment. She stood by the door, squatted, and then pissed all over the battered rug.

She retrieved her phone and was surprised to see that the battery wasn't completely dead. She noticed that she had a few texts.

Mike: Hey baby, Flo is gone. I wanna see you.

Me: Meet me at Anacostia Station, I need a HUGE favor!

***

"Hold the fuck up! So you're the one his goons been talking 'bout finding over in Southeast?"

"Guilty."

Tomorrow laughed carelessly. She pulled her maxi dress over her head and walked over to the closet to locate her sandals.

"He got niggas looking for two big Jeffrey Dahmer ass niggas, and the whole time, it's you?" Mishon yelled.

"Yep."

"Well, what about those dead cats all over his car? I know you ain't kill 'em?!"

Tomorrow smiled.

"Bitch, please tell me you didn't!"

"Mishon, what are razor blades for? Besides, that muthafucka better be lucky I didn't slice his dog the fuck up and spread it on top of his car instead. Girrrl, you should've seen that damn critter, it was ancient as hell."

Mishon wore a concerned look. Tomorrow seemed unaffected by the crime she had committed and Mishon just

155

didn't understand how she could be so calm about being held hostage for the weekend.

Hearing Tomorrow's story only made Mishon more confused. She wasn't sure what was going on with her best friend, but she had an odd feeling that perhaps Legacy's story wasn't all made up.

Mishon didn't want to alarm Tomorrow by acting as if something was wrong, so she tried her best to play it cool. She noticed Tomorrow at the mirror about to apply her makeup and decided to help out.

Mishon walked over to where Tomorrow stood.

"Sit down, ho. Lemme help." Mishon playfully grabbed the foundation from Tomorrow's hands.

Tomorrow sat down in the chair and allowed Mishon to get to work. Mishon decided to dig for a little more information about Quan.

She thought Tomorrow was crazy for handling Quan on her own and wanted to know what plans she had to rectify the situation. Mishon knew that Quan would not go away peacefully.

"What the fuck do you plan to do when he get out of the hospital?" Mishon inquired.

"He still gotta heal up. He'll be limping around for a while," Tomorrow joked.

"Do you need for me to holla at Brandon and Rico for you? I'm pretty sure they know Quan real good."

"Nah, I got this, but thanks anyway. He deserved it, Shon. The nigga took advantage of me and I had to handle it. He's embarrassed. He's not gonna come after me right away, especially if he got niggas thinking he was jumped," Tomorrow explained.

"Look," she continued. "I know you feel like you don't know me anymore, but you do. I'm still the same person,"

Tomorrow assured Mishon.

She handed Mishon her black eyeliner to apply next.

Yeah, bitch, only when you're heavily medicated, Mishon thought.

Mishon decided to change the subject. It was apparent that Tomorrow was unaffected by everything she had been through, and honestly, Mishon just didn't know what to say. Perhaps it was best that she just dropped the situation.

She decided that she didn't want to hear another word about Quan or the details of the crime. Maybe Legacy really did find funny medication in Tomorrow's purse. There were so many thoughts running through Mishon's mind and it was all too much for her to handle. Staying out of the situation was her best option, at least for now.

"If you say so. Well, I'm done with your eyeliner. How you like it?" Mishon asked.

She handed Tomorrow a mirror. Tomorrow flirted with her reflection. Mishon gave her an awkward glare before walking into the bathroom to clean the makeup residue from her hands.

I can't believe this bitch is so calm about being held hostage, Mishon thought to herself while putting Tomorrow's makeup back into the makeup bag.

She wanted to say more to Tomorrow about what Legacy had told her, but she knew that opening a new can of worms would not be the right thing to do just yet, not during their vacation.

She figured that if Tomorrow knew that Legacy was spreading rumors about her, she might suffer a similar fate as Quan, or maybe even the same fate as those cats.

Mishon loved Tomorrow like a sister and didn't want to judge her based on something she couldn't completely control. She didn't know the facts of her so-called mental illness and didn't want to assume anything. She also didn't want to be an accomplice to any crimes, so she decided to just play it cool. Besides, Tomorrow couldn't be that bad, could she?

"Damn, Shon, you gave me some thick cat eyes," Tomorrow joked.

"Oh girl, stop it! You know you wanna get all cute for your boo anyway."

"My boo? Explain?" Tomorrow giggled while still admiring her reflection.

"Don't think that I ain't notice you and Chris getting real close. Got that nigga Kane up in here pissed the fuck off."

"Yeah, we are. But we're taking our time with it. No rush. But I can care less about Kane. The fact that he brought his girl along on this vacay furthermore proves to me that I don't need to fuck with him like that no more."

Mishon walked back over to Tomorrow and applied clear lip gloss to her lips, adding the finishing touch.

"Perfect," Mishon said.

"Indeed I am." Tomorrow giggled and puckered up at her reflection.

"I'm 'bout to ride to the mall. I need to relax and do what I do."

"That's what's up. Let me grab my purse and sunglasses and we can ride."

Tomorrow and Mishon walked out of the bedroom and into the living room. Everyone seemed to be preoccupied with something. Legacy and Kane were watching basketball while Chris and Brandon were on the balcony smoking.

"We goin' to the mall. If y'all wanna roll, I suggest you get your shit together," Mishon announced as she headed to the balcony to speak with Brandon.

"I ain't goin' if she is!" Legacy protested. She looked directly at Tomorrow.

"Good, bitch, cuz I would prefer not to see your face

anyway." Tomorrow replied. She turned and faced Kane with a seductive stare.

"But how 'bout you Kane? I bet you'd like to go right?"

"Yeah, I'll ride, ain't got shit else to do. Just let me go and grab my wallet and a shirt."

Kane stood up and stretched before walking into the den.

"Kane! How the fuck you gon' just leave me here like that?" Legacy screamed.

She didn't want Kane anywhere near Tomorrow. She knew that he didn't give a damn about her feelings, but something in her still expected him to decline the offer.

"Legacy, you just said that you ain't wanna go. You ain't my keepa. Shit, you barely my girl. I don't need you to tell me what the fuck I can or cannot do! Oh, and I'm taking the money you gave me."

Tomorrow laughed. Kane got a kick out of embarrassing Legacy, especially since she was the one usually embarrassing him.

"And there aint shit you gonna do about it," Kane added before leaving the room to get ready.

Tomorrow watched as Kane left to make sure that she and Legacy were alone. Slowly, she trotted over to where Legacy sat and whispered:

"Don't worry. I'm not going to fuck your man on the trip. I'll be nice and wait 'til we get back to VA."

She paused and watched as Legacy grew infuriated.

"Until then, he's all yours, honey."

Mishon walked in from the balcony. She knew that something bad had gone down by the way Tomorrow and Legacy looked at each other with spiteful eyes.

"Aight. I'm ready now, I just had to holla at Brandon real quick. What's going on in here?" Mishon inquired with a raised eyebrow.

"Oh, nothing," Tomorrow sang. "Little Miss Sunshine here decided not to go, but her man is going. Now she's gonna sit here and twiddle her thumbs and continue to look dumb as fuck in them cheap ass Walmart pajamas," she added.

"You keep it up, ho," Legacy threatened.

Tomorrow shot Legacy a look of death before walking towards the door. Kane left the den and the two of them headed towards Mishon's car.

After Mishon put on her sunglasses and lip gloss, she looked over at Legacy, who was still sitting on the couch with a smug look on her face.

"Look, Legacy, if you want to go, you better put your feelings aside and come the fuck on here, cuz I'm 'bout to pull off. Are you sure you don't wanna go?"

Legacy didn't answer. She sat in silence wondering why Kane would just leave her behind the way he did. Her face was bare of expression. You could tell that she was in a deep thought, but she didn't say a word.

"Okay, sit here and look crazy. I'm gone."

Mishon walked out of the condo and joined Tomorrow and Kane.

Legacy turned and watched Chris and Brandon on the balcony.

I'mma have to up the ante on this bitch. She not taking me serious at all!

CHAPTER

~ 15 ~

Mishon and Tomorrow's first stop was Jones New York. Although the girls didn't know their way around the mall, finding their favorite shops was never an issue. Kane was definitely not feeling Mishon and Tomorrow's choice of stores, so he decided that he would just do his own thing.

"I'mma head over to Foot Locker and see what's up. Tomorrow, just hit my cell up when y'all about to leave so we can meet back up," Kane said.

"Yeah, okay."

Tomorrow eagerly brushed off Kane. She was glad that he had decided to separate from them because there was a lot she wanted to gossip freely about without holding anything back. She and Mishon continued to browse through the clothes racks.

"Now that that nigga decided to shoo fly, fill me in on you and Chris," Mishon insisted.

"Hmph, that nigga think he know me. I haven't given him any yet, though. He's different from the rest of the niggas I'm used to fuckin' wit'. But iono, I'm just going with the flow. You know how I do."

"I think he really fuck wit' you hard, but what you gon' do about Kane?"

"Girl, I told you, he's old news. Especially now. I still don't understand why he brought that bitch to Ocean City. She's been getting on my last damn nerve since she walked over the fucking threshold. It's clear he needs her for monetary reasons, but must we all suffer? I mean, damn! And this bitch is really on my shit list," Tomorrow professed.

She pulled a black hoop earring out of her purse and handed it to Mishon.

"Look what I found in my bedroom the other night."

"Oooh! This looks like Legacy's earring. You know she was sportin' joints just like that at Trell's party, right? Thinking she was the flyest chick in there." Mishon laughed.

"Girl, we wouldn't be caught dead wearing plastic earrings from Claire's, so I know that bitch was in my house, but the question is how the fuck she get in?"

"Damn, you think she broke in?"

"I can't call it, but my mom would have said that bitch stopped by, and she never would have allowed her past the damn door. That bitch tried to pull a James Bond move." Tomorrow laughed.

"But on the real, Shon, you already know how I feel about people being in my room, right? That bitch has gone too far."

"Yep, shit, she's definitely busted now! Why does she keep acting like nobody knows what she's up to? That bitch is sneaky." Mishon added.

"Why was she even in there?"

"Iono, but I'm gonna find out. I'm the wrong one to fuck with."

"Shit is crazy. Kane's ass needs to grow some dick hair and put that ho in her place."

"Umm-hmm," Tomorrow said while trying on a sexy pair of pumps.

"Do you see how she be punkin' him?"

"Oh yeah, but you know how Legacy is. She's always treated him like shit even when they first got together. Now that she knows about you two sleepin' together, it's like she's really on some get back type shit. Sneaking in your house and shit."

"Well, if she knew better, she would do better, cuz that bitch doesn't have the slightest clue who she's fucking with," Tomorrow declared.

Mishon watched as Tomorrow paused and applied more of her Scarlet Rouge lipstick. Instantly, thoughts came rolling back from her conversation with Legacy and the news report that she had just seen a few weeks ago. She shook her head in hopes of removing the uncalming doubt.

"Damn, why are you looking at me like that?" Tomorrow laughed.

"No reason, I was lost in my own thoughts," Mishon lied.

"Oh, well snap out of it, trick. By the way, remind me to stop at the drugstore before we leave. I gotta pick up a few things."

CHAPTER

~ 16 ~

*B*randon had been feeling a lot better. Since the girls were gone, he and Chris decided to play video games on the big screen in the den. Legacy sat on the couch in the living room waiting for Kane to return. She watched Brandon and Chris closely as she plotted her scheme.

"Finally, a nigga get to chill. Mishon done had a nigga rippin' and runnin' since we got here. Since this is the last night, I'mma chill the fuck out, ya dig?"

"Shit, y'all might as well be married," Chris chuckled.

"I ain't ready for that ball 'n' chain just yet, but shit, you never know. But speaking of relationships, my nig, how you feelin' 'bout Tomorrow? I mean, you been shackin' up with her all week."

"We been bunnin' up a lot and having some real deep conversations. I wanna say it's nothing too serious just yet, but I'd be lying. She's smart, sexy and got mad swag. I'm digging that shit. I hope to spend more time with her once we get back around our way, but you know how it goes. We'll see."

"Yeah, she's real cool people," Brandon chimed in.

Legacy overheard the entire conversation and couldn't help but interrupt.

"What the fuck ever!" She blurted out, attempting to capture their attention.

Brandon and Chris both looked over their shoulders. Brandon shook his head and paused the game.

"Ahhh shit! If it ain't the mommy to be. Why didn't you take your ass to the mall?" Brandon questioned.

"I'm pretty sure you know the reason, Brandon," she answered as she walked into the den where the guys were.

Chris laughed. He wasn't sure why everybody treated Legacy so terribly, but he thought it was hilarious.

"Yo Brandon, why y'all always carrying that girl like that?"

Brandon pulled out the half of blunt he had saved from earlier and put it to his lips. Legacy pulled up a chair next to the guys and sat down like she was a part of the conversation.

"Man, you ain't been around long enough to understand. She got mouth! A reckless ass mouth!" Brandon informed Chris.

"Why do you care?" Legacy said. "And Chris, you should prolly be worried about why your girl fucking my man instead of trying to figure me out," Legacy defended herself.

"See what I mean? She don't know how to chill. Always on level ten when she need to bring that shit down to about a three."

"Hahaha, so chick be wildin', huh?" Chris asked Brandon as if Legacy wasn't in the room.

"Nigga, I swear, she will have your ass ready to slap the shit outta her. Either that or sue that ass for mental anguish and shit."

Brandon cut the game off and shook his head at how childish Legacy could be. He didn't understand why Mishon and Tomorrow even wasted their time playing nice with her. She was confrontational, immature, and it was clear that she was a hater. Brandon just didn't get it.

He passed the blunt to Chris and walked into the kitchen to find something to eat. Chris and Legacy followed closely behind.

"Shit, I'm 'bout to cook, y'all want some grill cheese and bacon sandwiches?"

"Make me two, my nig."

Chris turned on the TV and sat down on the sofa in the living room.

"No thanks," Legacy answered before sitting in a chair across from Chris.

While Brandon cooked, Legacy decided to indulge in conversation with Chris. She wanted to know just how into Tomorrow he was and secretly wondered what she could do to make sure they didn't get any closer. Tomorrow had ruined her relationship, so why shouldn't she have the chance to seek revenge?

"So Chris, what makes you think you know Tomorrow so well?"

Legacy overheard Chris and Brandon's entire conversation on the balcony, but Chris didn't want to discuss his business openly, especially not with someone like Legacy. He changed the subject.

167

"Girl, do you smoke?"

"No, I have asthma," Legacy replied.

She proudly removed an inhaler from her pocket and waved it in the air.

Chris laughed.

"Here, go head. Take a pull, just one."

Chris put the blunt up to Legacy's lips and held it there. She deeply inhaled and took one long hit before she began to cough uncontrollably.

"Eas—easy girl, damn. You sure you ain't smoke before?" Chris joked.

"Nah, I ain't really into that like everybody else is." She coughed.

Brandon finally finished making the grill cheese sandwiches. He fixed himself a plate and walked into the den, hoping to watch some college basketball and vibe out without disruptions.

"Yo, Chris, the food is done." Brandon signaled to Chris.

Without warning, Legacy jumped up and headed towards the kitchen. She began to fix Chris' plate.

"I'll get it for you," she insisted.

In Legacy's mind, she had already won. Her warped reality told her that Chris was undoubtedly interested in her, and since she knew that Tomorrow wanted him, the ball was in her court.

Brandon was caught off guard by Legacy's actions. He looked at Chris with a confused face, and then walked back into the den. Chris quickly jumped up and walked behind him.

"Chris do you see that shit?" Brandon laughed.

"She took a hit off the jay."

"Oh shit! For real? That chick be fakin', acting like she pregnant and shit."

168

Legacy entered the room and handed Chris his plate. She sat down across from him.

"Here you go, sweetie."

"Thanks," Chris said dryly.

"So what y'all niggas up to after this?"

Chris yawned. He took a small bite of the sandwich, but he couldn't get really relaxed with Legacy staring dead at him.

Brandon just ignored her. She was getting a little too weird for him and he didn't want to be the reason why Mishon whooped her ass.

"I'mma go lay down after I'm done eating. Nigga still fucked up off all that drinkin' we was doin' last night." He yawned.

Brandon and Chris continued to watch the game. Legacy attempted to spark more conversation and draw attention to herself, but the guys were unconsumed. But like always, she continued to talk and ignored the fact that they were not interested in holding a conversation with her. In fact, they both just wanted her to shut the hell up.

Eventually, Brandon got fed up with hearing her voice and decided to put on Nas' "Illmatic." He turned it all the way up to the max volume.

"You smacked and you only took one hit?"

"Yea, I am feeling good," Legacy said while rubbing her arms.

Her eyes were low and she felt like she was on a "Voyage to Atlantis." But instead of just relaxing, her weed intake only heightened her annoyance.

Nearly an hour had passed, and Legacy still wouldn't let up. She was rambling on about how Kane didn't deserve her and that she was going to find a man who could really handle being in a serious relationship.

Brandon continued to ignore her as he vibed out to Nas' classic sounds. He closed his eyes and slowly nodded, absorbing every lyric. Chris had dozed off in his chair. Lucky for him, he no longer had to deal with Legacy's annoying voice.

During the middle of the Illmatic album, Brandon felt a sharp pain in his stomach. He discovered that eating a greasy grilled cheese and bacon sandwich was not the right cure for bubble guts.

"Yo Chris! Chris! Damn, that nigga is knocked out," Brandon yelled.

He tried his best to wake Chris because he didn't trust Legacy. He knew she would try something crazy, but he just couldn't fight the urge to go to the bathroom. Although he knew he'd regret leaving his friend alone with her, he ran out the den as quickly as he could and made his way to the nearest toilet.

Legacy watched Chris closely. He was slouched down in his chair unaffected by his surroundings. He fell in and out of sleep, but it was obvious that he'd soon be headed straight for cloud nine.

She decided that she would spring her plan into action. Chris had to be into her. She could tell by the way that he looked at her when he spoke.

Chris was really the only person who had paid Legacy any attention since they arrived at Ocean City. He really listened to her, something that Kane had never done or cared to do. She understood why Tomorrow was so into him. The brother was smooth. But she wanted to see exactly what had Tomorrow all sprung. Now Tomorrow would know how it felt to be betrayed.

The speakers were bumping Nas' "Memory Lane" and Legacy's new high took complete control.

She slowly sashayed over to Chris and got on her knees. She softly fondled his dick, but he didn't respond. Chris was knocked out cold. Without a word, Legacy unbuckled his jeans and pulled his dick from his shorts.

Her eyes grew wide when she realized how endowed Chris was. She definitely wouldn't give up the chance to test him out now.

Legacy slammed her mouth down onto his dick and began sucking it like her life depended on it. Chris' eyes immediately shot open, and for a second, he was stunned. He couldn't believe that Legacy was that bold.

He quickly jumped up and pushed Legacy to the floor.

"Bitch, is you crazy? What the fuck you doin?" he yelled.

Normally, Chris would've been down for something like that, but the way that he felt about Tomorrow was undeniable, and he just wouldn't allow anything to ruin that.

He had finally met someone who was on his level, someone who sparked his imagination as well as his sexual appetite. Why would he ruin it all over a little head? Especially when Legacy didn't have a clue what she was doing. Her skills were mediocre at best.

Mishon, Tomorrow and Kane pulled up in the driveway. After a long day of shopping, they were more than eager to get back and show off their purchases.

The ladies exited the car and headed for the condo. Kane stayed behind to grab all of the bags.

"What's wrong?" Mishon asked as they walked up to the door of the condo.

Mishon looked at her friend and noticed that something was up. Tomorrow wore an awkward expression and it made her a little uneasy.

"Iono, I just feel weird," Tomorrow replied while pulling her drink from her bag.

She tried to escape the unsettling feeling in her stomach, but it just wouldn't let up.

Tomorrow took a sip of her Snapple and opened the door, and Mishon followed closely behind.

Legacy wasn't giving in. She still had Chris' dick in her hand, clutching it every time he tried to get away.

"I can suck dick way better than Tomorrow can," she teased.

She reached up in an attempt to get one last taste of Chris' forbidden nectar.

"Yall niggas is ill wit' the game!" Mishon yelled.

The unexpected sounds of her loud screams shocked Chris and Legacy back into reality. They both jumped like they had just seen a ghost. Chris zipped up his pants and anxiously stood to his feet, but Legacy refused to move from her compromising position. She hadn't expected them to return so soon, but she was glad that Tomorrow had caught her in the act. In fact, she was downright thrilled.

Mishon took off her shades at stared at them. She was enraged. She simply couldn't believe that they'd be sitting in the middle of the living room doing something so raunchy. Mishon knew that the spectacle before her had to be Legacy's doing. Chris enjoyed his privacy. There was no way he'd just allow that to go down out in the open.

Tomorrow stood there in silence clutching her Snapple. Instantly, she thought of murderous ways to kill both Chris and Legacy without being caught. She had a right to be mad. Chris wasn't hers, but that didn't stop her from feeling the sting of betrayal. Most of all, she felt embarrassed, and that feeling only made her angrier.

Legacy finally got off her knees and grinned at Tomorrow. She wiped the corners of her mouth with her fingers for the added affect and crossed her arms as if she had no worries in the world.

Mishon went to the Stereo and knocked if off the shelf, breaking the whole system. When Brandon heard the shatter, he came running out of the bathroom.

"Legacy, what the fuck?!" Mishon screamed.

"Yeah, I did it! I sucked Tomorrow's man off and his cum tasted good," Legacy taunted.

"Nah, Tomorrow, it ain't what it looked like. This bitch is crazy!" Chris struggled to buckle his jeans.

At that moment, Chris hated Legacy. He knew that he would have hell trying to explain all of this to Tomorrow. He knew what it looked like to the average person, but there was no way he would have allowed it to go down had he been fully awake. Choosing Legacy over Tomorrow, that just would never happen.

Chris didn't want Tomorrow to think that he was like all the rest of the dudes that she had encountered in the past. He knew that Tomorrow would assume that he was full of game, and she'd quickly build back the walls that he had been fighting so hard to tear down.

Mishon walked into the den to inspect the scenery. She didn't know why she was so upset, but the anger she felt was real. Legacy didn't try to sleep with Brandon, but for her, it was about the principle. She knew she should have never allowed Legacy into their condo in the first place.

"Uh huh, y'all niggas up in here eating grilled cheese sandwiches, smoking jays and blasting music and shit! Looks like the perfect fuck scene to me."

"You gonna pay for that shit you just broke, Mishon!" Brandon yelled as he picked up his stereo off the floor.

"Nigga, fuck your stereo! How you gon' let this shit go down while we ain't here?" Mishon screamed back while kicking it against the wall.

"Nah, fuck that! Your girl Legacy planned that shit!" Brandon angrily replied.

He grabbed Mishon by the arms and shook her. He needed her to calm down so that everyone else could figure out what was going on.

CRASH!

Everyone paused and instantly became silent when they heard the noise. Tomorrow stood there with fire in her eyes. Her hand bled uncontrollably and shattered glass hit the floor in pieces.

"See, I told y'all that bitch was crazy!" Legacy yelled.

"She done broke that bottle with her bare hand."

Kane walked into the condo carrying all the shopping bags. He didn't realize that he had just stepped into a battle zone. He noticed that Tomorrow's hand was bleeding, and the blood was dripping on the floor.

"Oh shit!"

Kane dropped the bags by the door, grabbed Tomorrow by the arm and led her into the kitchen.

"Nah, I got it Kane, back up," Chris said while tugging on her other arm.

Tomorrow pushed Chris aside and walked into the kitchen with Kane. He ran cold water over her hand and wrapped it up in the kitchen towel.

Chris ran to the kitchen behind them. He felt like he should have been the one to console Tomorrow.

"Can we talk please?" Chris asked.

"Now is not a good time," Tomorrow answered.

She tried not to look at Chris. She felt that tingling in her belly, that tingle that told her to kill, but she knew she had to resist it. Tomorrow needed to be as far away from him as possible before she ended up doing something she'd soon regret.

Kane ran to his room and retrieved his mini firs aid kit. Luckily the cuts weren't too deep, so cleaning Tomorrow up would be easy. He grabbed the kit and led Tomorrow into her bedroom. She sat on her bed while he wrapped her hand up.

Legacy pranced around the house and acted as if nothing had occurred. She was glad that Tomorrow caught her in the act. At least now Tomorrow would know that she wasn't an amateur when it came to payback.

"Now that bitch knows what it feels like. Stupid trick!" Legacy blurted.

She stretched out on the couch and wrapped herself up in a blanket. Legacy was enjoying her revenge on Tomorrow. There was no remorse on her face, only a look of accomplishment.

"Oh no, ho!" Mishon interrupted her moment of glory.

She pulled Legacy from the couch, causing her fake ponytail piece to fly across the room.

"Your ass gotta get the fuck up outta here!"

"Get her off me! Get her the fuck off me!" Legacy screamed in pain.

"That's real fucked up, Mishon. You taking this bipolar bitch's side instead of mine? She been fucking Kane for how long, but everybody wanna get mad at me for sucking a nigga dick who ain't even really her man?"

"Bitch, fuck you. Kane never really wanted yo' ass. He's been using you and he dumped you weeks ago, bitch! That's the fucking difference!" Mishon screamed.

Brandon and Chris grabbed Mishon by the arms and dragged her into the den to sit down.

Mishon warned Legacy at the beginning of the trip not to start any drama, but she refused to listen. She knew that Tomorrow was wrong for sleeping with Kane, but in the words of Jay-Z: *"You don't get a nigga back like that."*

Kane never really liked Legacy, he had simply settled for second, or third, best. So in Mishon's mind, Kane never really belonged to Legacy. Besides, everyone knew Kane only stayed for the car and the money.

Legacy knew how much Tomorrow and Chris liked each other, so trying something with him, especially when her own so-called "boyfriend" was there on the trip, was simply unacceptable.

Mishon decided that since Tomorrow wasn't normally the type to get hyped up, she would do enough for the both of them. Little did she know, Tomorrow could hold her own and didn't need any back up.

Tomorrow may not have been overly animated, but she was undoubtedly calculated in her actions. Sometimes she allowed her emotions to interfere, but for the most part, when she was on a mission, her treachery was unmatched by most. Her nonchalant attitude was only a cover up for the havoc she would soon cause.

After seeing Tomorrow break that glass with her bare hands and not flinch, Mishon realized that Tomorrow was indeed capable of doing everything that she'd allegedly done to Quan. She'd never admit it aloud, but that made her a bit fearful of what Tomorrow was capable of. In her heart, she knew that Tomorrow would never do her harm, but she couldn't escape the feeling that her best friend had become someone she barely knew.

"Calm the fuck down!" Brandon ordered. "Matter of fact, everybody shut the fuck up!"

Kane walked out of Tomorrow's bedroom to grab a bucket of ice. He walked past Legacy, not giving her a chance to explain.

"I don't give a fuck about you, Kane! Your dick ain't

176

nowhere near as big as his." Legacy pointed to Chris.

"Legacy, you better shut the fuck up," Chris said. "Bitch, I swear to fucking you gonna get dealt wit when we get back in town, bitch!" Chris shook his head back and forth.

He followed Kane back to Tomorrow's room. Chris needed to talk to her and thought that it would be the perfect time, but when he reached the room, Kane slammed the door in his face and locked it.

Chris wanted to break down the door and smack the shit out of Kane, but decided against it. There was already way too much drama going on.

He stood next to the door and tried to get his thoughts together. He hoped that Tomorrow would give him a chance to explain himself.

"Here, I got some ice that'll help to bring down the swelling a lil' bit," Kane said, standing over Tomorrow's bed.

"Thanks a lot."

"What the fuck was Legacy thinking? That bitch is gonna come across the wrong one and get hurt one day."

"Hmph, yeah you're right. She is going to come across the wrong one."

"You gon' need a pain reliever. I think I got some Advil in my bag."

"Nah, that's okay. Trust me, I got that on lock."

After Kane finished caring for Tomorrow's hand, he sat down on the bed next to her. He put his hand on her face and caressed her cheek.

Tomorrow became annoyed. She wasn't in the mood for any of Kane's horny little tricks. She knew what he wanted, but he definitely wasn't going to get it. Not from her anyway.

Dear Lord, please remove his pudgy fingers from my face before I bite them off and eat 'em.

"Look Kane, thank you for lookin' out, but I just wanna

177

be alone right now."

"Really? Do you really want me to go?"

"Do I need to spell it out for you? G-O please, just go," she said while pointing to the door.

Kane sighed. He thought that taking care of Tomorrow would make her see that he was really the one she needed to be with.

He looked back and noticed she wasn't even looking in his direction anymore.

"Do you really, really want me to go?" Kane asked.

"Kane, get the fuck out!" Tomorrow screamed.

Before Kane walked out the door he stopped and looked back.

"You know, you are so fucking ungrateful and stuck up! How could anybody put up with your selfish ass?"

Tomorrow was enraged. Kane was definitely barking up the wrong tree at the wrong damn time.

"You know what, I'm tired of your dumb ass! You are so lame! No car! No job! You think the good dick is gonna keep you afloat forever? Do me a favor and stop hanging from my clit. Your bitch is that bitch in the living room with the jacked up ponytail. Go see about that ho and leave me the fuck alone!"

"Fuck you!"

"You wish, huh?" Tomorrow laughed.

Kane walked out and slammed the door behind him, but Tomorrow wasn't concerned about making Kane mad; she had bigger fish to fry. She couldn't stop thinking about what Legacy had done, but she would surely show her exactly who had the upper hand.

Tomorrow grabbed her purse off the bed and pulled out a plastic bag. It was time to let Legacy really see how the game was played.

She opened the door and noticed Chris leaning up

against the wall, but Tomorrow acted as if she didn't see him.

Silence fell over the den as she approached. Legacy stood up against the wall and everyone stared in Tomorrow's direction. Nobody could figure out why she was smiling at a time like this, and it made them nervous. What was about to happen?

"You okay, girl, how's your hand?" Mishon asked while sitting on the couch under Brandon's watch.

"It's good," Tomorrow quickly replied. "Hey Legacy, no hard feelings. I mean, I get it. I did fuck your man and I was wrong. My bad."

Tomorrow turned to Legacy with a look of regret, but Legacy's face only revealed confusion. She couldn't believe that Tomorrow was actually trying to give somewhat of an apology. Everyone else's face showed that they were equally as confused.

"I felt so bad that I rushed out earlier just to get you a gift. Since we all know you're expecting, I wanted to show my support. Congrats. Here, open it!" Tomorrow smiled.

No one moved. Everyone stood shocked by Tomorrow's sudden niceness, especially when she had just seen Legacy slurping on Chris' manhood. No one knew what to expect, so they remained silent and watched the show.

Legacy was nervous. Anything could have been in that bag, and she wasn't really sure how to take Tomorrow's apology. Was she sincere? Or was this simply another ploy?

She took the bag out of Tomorrow's hand and pulled out the gift. Everyone nervously waited to see what Tomorrow had purchased.

Tomorrow chuckled as Legacy mouthed the words EPT: Error Proof Test.

"A fucking pregnancy test, trick?" Legacy screamed.

"Well, I figured you should take the test to lay all this fake pregnancy shit to rest once and for all, bitch!" Tomorrow said boldly.

"Oh, and it's an EPT two-pack, so don't worry about taking both right now. You may want to save the other one for the next time you wanna fake a pregnancy," she continued.

Everyone laughed.

"Bitch, I ain't got to take shit! I don't have to prove nothing to none of y'all losers. Stupid muthafuckas!"

Legacy threw the pregnancy test on the floor.

"You got something to prove to me!" Kane chimed in. "You been stringing this charade along for a while now. Now, if you don't take it for nobody else, at least take it for me."

"Suck my ass, nigga, I ain't taking shit! Y'all all a buncha lowlives. You bitches ain't shit, especially you, Tomorrow. I'm leaving this wack ass condo! Kane, if you going, you better get your shit!"

"Bitch, I ain't goin'! You rollin' solo, ho! I'm tired of your ass! All you do is talk. Somebody should cut your fucking tongue out, you lil' bald-headed bitch!"

Sounds tempting. Tomorrow giggled to herself.

"That's right, Kane. Shit, it's about time you put her ass in check," Mishon yelled.

Legacy felt defeated. She grabbed some of her things from the den. She wanted to hurry up and get out of Ocean City. It was apparent that she no longer had friends there, and it was all because of Tomorrow.

Kane and Brandon decided to be nice gentlemen and assist Legacy by throwing her things out the door and into the hallway.

Everyone was completely fed up with Legacy's antics. She had to go. She had ruined a perfectly good trip, and no one wanted any more to do with her.

"Stop it! Don't touch my stuff!" Legacy screamed while fishing for her shoes over the hallway banister.

"You gonna regret this!" she threatened.

Brandon shut the door and locked it.

"Ding dong, that bitch is dead!" Kane yelled.

"Well, I guess she didn't want her gift." Tomorrow shrugged.

"Bitch, you are crazy. I can't believe you pulled out the EPT on that ho. That was honestly a classic fuckin' moment!" Mishon gasped.

"I told you. She just don't have a clue who she fuckin' with."

Everyone sighed in relief.

"Finally, some peace and quiet. A nigga gotta go finish what he started in the bathroom. I'll see y'all later. Don't forget the bonfire is at eight. Be ready," Brandon joked before rushing back to the bathroom.

Mishon followed closely behind. She knew that she and Brandon would have a lot to discuss in private.

Everyone retreated to their rooms to get some rest before the bonfire. Kane went into the den and Tomorrow headed back down the hall, ignoring Chris as she passed by. She knew that Chris would follow her, but she didn't want to talk. She entered her bedroom and locked the door behind her.

"Yo, Tomorrow? Open up! Please, I need to holla at you."

"No."

"Let me explain."

"That's okay. I saw all I needed to see."

"Ugh! Well at least let me get some sleep like I was tryna do earlier."

"Sofa bed," Tomorrow replied nonchalantly.

Chris begged for nearly fifteen minutes before Tomorrow finally opened the door. She got back into the bed and threw a pillow in between her and Chris to make sure there was no touching.

"Mari?"

"You think those lil nick names gonna make this shit better? My name is Tomorrow, **not** Mari. Don't say another word to me. Just go to sleep like you said you was gonna do. Understood?"

"Fuck it then."

"Good."

They both remained in silence for nearly ten minutes, but Chris just couldn't resist the urge to speak.

"So you not gonna let me explain for real?"

"You gon' be sleepin' on that sofa bed in a minute."

"This shit is crazy." Chris rolled over.

He wanted to know what she was thinking, but he knew there would be no getting through to her right now. Emotions were still running high, and honestly, he didn't blame her. If the shoe had been on the other foot, he probably would have been upset too. Hell, he would have probably gone to jail after bashing someone's face in.

Chris figured he would give Tomorrow her space and try his hand again later at the bonfire. But for now, he needed to finish up that nap he had attempted earlier.

CHAPTER

~ 17 ~

fter all of the crazy drama that had taken place, everyone settled into normalcy. Legacy was gone and the morale of the entire group had magically lifted. Although there were unsettled issues between Tomorrow and Chris, they remained civil for the sake of the group.

A few hours had passed since the huge blow up, and everyone decided that it would be best to attend the Ocean City Spring Break Bonfire that would take place that night. It was their last night and they wanted to have a memorable moment that didn't involve breaking glasses and pregnancy tests.

There were tons of other college students enjoying their vacation at Ocean City as well. The bonfire was everyone's chance to meet and greet and enjoy their final night. Everyone was dressed in their swimwear, ready to have a great time on the beach.

As soon as they reached the sand, Mishon and Brandon went their own separate way. They wanted to enjoy their last night together without any interruptions. Tomorrow watched as Brandon scooped up Mishon and jokingly tossed her into the water.

She laughed.

She could hear Mishon complaining about her hair and how he was going to pay for her to get it redone. Tomorrow was happy for Mishon and Brandon's love, but she was sad over her own failed attempt at a relationship. She truly thought that Chris could've been the one for her, but like so many other times before, she was disappointed.

It was much bigger than Chris hooking up with Legacy. She was hurt about the fact that she had allowed him to get into her mind and slowly seep into her heart in a matter of days.

Tomorrow wanted to harm Chris for making her feel emotions that she had once refused. She thought about all the things that she could do to make both him and Legacy pay for crossing her. There was one thing for sure: Legacy had to die.

Chris had unknowingly been a part of Legacy's ploy to destroy Tomorrow, and she planned to make her pay for all of it.

A smile brushed across her face. Tomorrow had the perfect plan to make sure that Legacy would never breathe again.

She removed her shoes and dug her feet into the sand. That was always her favorite thing to do whenever she visited the beach. In a life full of lies and deceit, Tomorrow seemed to always be content with the simple things. She may have looked for acceptance in all of the wrong places, but she found solace in those things that came easy.

Something as simple as digging her feet in the sand made her forget about all of her troubles, if only for the moment.

Chris watched Tomorrow from the boardwalk. He could see her sitting in the sand enjoying some alone time. He couldn't resist the need to be close to her. He had to explain what happened with Legacy and he needed to do it soon.

He walked up behind her and heard Tomorrow humming a tune. He stood stunned for a moment. Her voice was beautiful and it instantly put on a smile on his face.

"I didn't know you could sing, shawty," Chris said, interrupting Tomorrow's song.

"There's a lot of things you don't know about me."

"Yeah? Like what?"

"Why? It's not like it matters now anyway."

Tomorrow jumped up from the sand and walked away from Chris with her flip flops swinging in her left hand and holding the sides of her dress with her right.

Her earth tone beach dress effortlessly flowed in the wind, and her locs did the same. She looked like royalty as she moved along the sands.

Chris stood in awe of her black beauty. Her cocoa complexion glistened in the night's backdrop and she smelled like warm sugary vanilla.

He chuckled to himself when he noticed her irritated, smug expression. She was sexy even when she was completely pissed off.

He followed closely behind her in hopes of resolving their issues.

"Tomorrow, quit running away from what's real!" Chris yelled.

Tomorrow stopped in her tracks. She turned around

and looked Chris directly in the eyes. She had a mean look of contempt written across her face and decided to give him a piece of her mind.

"What's real? Nigga, I'll tell you what's real. Walking in and seeing that bitch sucking your dick. That's what's real!" Tomorrow shrieked.

She turned to walk away again, but this time, Chris stopped her. He grabbed her and held onto her arms.

"Listen. I'm only gon' say this shit one more time. That bitch set me up. I was sleep. As soon as I felt that shit, I woke up and pushed her off. That's what you walked in on. Me pushing that bitch off me. That's it. It's not something I wanted to happen. I don't like her, and I would never do nothing to fuck up what we got going on. I wanna be with you."

Deep down Tomorrow believed that Chris was telling the truth, but she was afraid that things were becoming way too serious between them and it scared her. Catching Chris with Legacy gave her the reason she needed to back off from him, even though her heart told her otherwise.

It was just too soon to be taking such a big leap, especially because she didn't know when the urge to kill would arise within her again.

"Look Chris, I just..." Tomorrow sighed.

"Can I share something serious with you?" Chris interrupted.

Before allowing Tomorrow to give an answer, Chris completed what he had to say. He was tired of running from love and wanted Tomorrow to know that he was willing to give them a real chance. No games, no lies, just two people who really care about each other in an attempt at something real.

Although the two had gotten close over the week, Chris was ready to truly open up to Tomorrow. He knew that he had to allow her into his world in order for him to be a part of hers.

He grabbed her by the hand and led her down to the shore. Tomorrow was reluctant to follow, but figured that she'd at least hear him out, especially since she planned to end whatever they had going on.

She watched as he inhaled deeply. Chris looked as if he had a heavy burden on his heart that he needed to release. Tomorrow knew that look all too well.

"Look, life ain't been no storybook fairytale for me, shawty." Chris paused.

He looked up and admired the midnight sky. Tomorrow wondered what he was thinking.

"No one's has, so what are you getting at?" she replied impatiently.

"Just listen. Don't talk. I need you just to listen."

"Okay."

"I'm originally from Brooklyn, grew up with my moms and pops. My pops was a hustla, jack of all trades. But he made most of his money from dealing and pimping. And my mother, well she was his bottom...you know. She was only seventeen when she found out she was pregnant with me. She wanted to get out of the game and hoped that a nigga would come with her. You know, for the sake of family, right?"

Tomorrow listened closely. She wasn't sure where his story was going, but it had already started to get good.

"Well, that ain't happen. Pops only knew one way of living, and the game was the only way for him. He allowed my mom to do the whole mommy thing for a while, but he had a motto: everyone in the house had to work in order to eat. Her thing was slanging pussy, and because she loved him, she decided to get back into it. My mom hoped every day that my pops would get it together and choose his family over the streets, but it just never happened. And she resented that nigga every day for it."

187

Chris paused and looked at Tomorrow with a stern look.

"Why are you telling me this, Chris?"

"I just need you to listen. Please," Chris begged.

Tomorrow sat quietly and allowed Chris to finish his story. She had a sneaking suspicion that the story wouldn't end well. She swallowed hard and Chris continued spilling the secrets of his life.

"One day, I came home from school. I was about 13 maybe, and I heard moms yelling at pops. She told him she was done with the game and was taking me away. I heard him telling her that she could leave, but there was no way that she was leaving with his only son. I watched as she packed her shit like she was really gonna leave. He ain't even pay her ass no mind. Matter of fact, if I can remember correctly, this nigga was laughing and calling her bluff."

Chris chuckled as he remembered the past.

"I watched from my room. The door was cracked and I peeped my eyes through the slit just enough to see what the fuck was going down. All he kept saying to her was *bitch, you ain't leaving and you ain't taking my son. Quit wasting your time.* I guess my moms got pissed cuz a nigga wasn't taking her seriously, and she just went off."

Chris swallowed the spit that had begun to form in his mouth. He wasn't sure of how accepting Tomorrow would be of his story, but he knew that if he wanted to be with her, there could be no more secrets.

"The next thing I know, she starts screaming nigga, *he ain't even your kid. That's right, nigga, he ain't yours. I been fucking other niggas for years, did you really think a limp dick ass nigga like you could actually produce viable sperm?* Pops flipped. He punched her so hard that I swear I saw her head spin. He knew she was lying, but I guess it was the principle of the shit. No man wants his manhood questioned or tested. He started choking her with his bare hands. Shawty, it felt like I was in the front row of a fucking movie. I watched my father go blank as he slowly strangled the life from my mother and showed no compassion. But it gets worse, he started fucking her right there in the living room after he killed her. The crazy nigga called the police himself and waited for 'em to come and take his ass away."

Tomorrow couldn't believe what she was hearing. Tears slowly began to form in her eyes when she noticed how the story affected Chris. She could tell he was getting quite emotional.

"I'm so sorry you had to go through that." Tomorrow grabbed Chris' hand and pulled him in for a hug.

"But when the police arrived, he was already dead. Gun shot to the head. They assumed it was a suicide."

"What do you mean *they assumed?*" Tomorrow eyes grew wide.

Was Chris telling her what she thought he was telling her? Had he killed his own father in a fit of rage?

"That was my moms, shawty," Chris replied without directly answering Tomorrow's question.

"So you…"

"Did what had to be done." He shook his head.

"Gotcha," Tomorrow replied.

She couldn't judge Chris for taking matters into his own hands. She had harmed innocent men with no regard. At least the body on Chris' hands deserved to die.

"Anyway. After that, I moved in with Brandon and my Auntie for a while. They ain't wanna see me go into the system, so they looked out. That's how I got to D.C. I had an aunt from here who took me in after that. But I've basically been on my own since I was 15. Needless to say, I don't trust many people, shawty."

Chris looked dead into Tomorrow's eyes. He wanted her to know that this story wasn't in vain. He had allowed her into a place that no one had ever seen before, and he wanted her to know that she was special to him.

"I told you that story not to get a fuckin' pity party, but because I don't want any secrets.

I want you to know I'm for real. You the first chick I ever told that fuckin' story too. As a matter of fact, you may only be like the fourth person who even knows."

"Damn, I don't even know what to say, Chris," Tomorrow replied.

"You ain't gotta say nothing. I just wanted you to know about me. I'mma real ass nigga and I would never intentionally do anything to harm or deceive you. I'm laying everything on the line, so the ball's in your court, shawty."

"I wanna share something with you too."

"Really?" Chris smiled.

"Yes. But not here, let's go back to the room."

Back at the condo, Tomorrow and Chris sat on the bed unsure of what to say to each other. Tomorrow knew that in order for her to truly give Chris a shot, she had to open up about her own past, a past that she fought every day to forget.

"I was raped, Chris. Back in Chicago, when I was like eight. By my dad's son, my half brother. I've blocked so many of the details out, but the nigga was like twenty-one at the time. My mother had left to go to work and he was supposed to be babysitting me."

Tomorrow lay back on the bed and peered at the ceiling. She knew that if she had to tell her story, she had to do it on her own terms.

"Do you know this nigga kissed me on the forehead after he stole my fucking innocence? This happened a handful of times. He would fuck me and then tell me if I ever told anyone, he'd kill me. But luckily, I didn't have to tell, cuz one day my mother came walking in when he was ripping my panties, and she went crazy. I've never seen my mother do no shit like that. She hurt him really bad."

Chris couldn't believe what he was hearing. How could anyone harm a child, especially their own flesh and blood? He felt the blood boil within him. How hadn't he picked up on it? Tomorrow's actions gave off clear indications that she had suffered a horrible past, but hearing that she was raped caught him completely off guard.

"I don't recall everything that went down after that because it's still a blur, but all I know is that night, our bags were packed and we were outta there. We moved to Virginia and started a whole new life. I haven't seen my brother or dad since. Last I heard, my brother had got arrested for raping another young girl and was serving time for that, and my dad is in jail for some murder. But I've literally been getting screwed by niggas my whole fuckin' life. Justice fucking served, right?"

Tomorrow laughed before spontaneously breaking down into tears. Chris had never seen Tomorrow so vulnerable, and it concerned him. He grabbed her and hugged her.

"I would never hurt you, shawty," Chris promised.

Tomorrow didn't reply. She allowed Chris to cuddle her in his arms, but she didn't say a word. She felt that maybe she had said too much. Too many emotions escaped her because she hadn't told that story to anyone other than her therapist. It felt good to finally release some tension, but it was also scary because it was a place that Tomorrow had never been. A place called Reality.

Deep inside, she knew that her urges to kill stemmed from those very secrets that she hid within herself. She knew she'd eventually have to tackle her problems head on, but it hurt too much to face them now. Tomorrow needed more time. The problem was she didn't know who else would end up dead by then.

"I'm serious, Tomorrow. You have me now, so you ain't gotta worry about another nigga hurting you. I'm always gon' be here. We got a crazy ass bond, it's hard not to see it. I know you feel it too. I ain't tryna rush it, but I want you to know that you always got me."

Chris kissed Tomorrow's lips. He immediately felt that same sensation he felt when he kissed her for the first time. They both felt it.

She allowed him to lay her back on the bed. After everything they had just shared, they knew that it was the perfect time to consummate the relationship. He stood up and admired her for awhile.

Chris had never actually made love to a woman. He had fucked plenty, but he never actually loved any of his previous partners. This time would be special.

He reached for his his iPod shuffle and placed in it the docking station. Silk's "Let's Make Love" rang throughout the room.

"What you know about this music, young buck? This that real music right here," Tomorrow joked as she snapped her fingers and sang along with the track.

"This was way before your time. Quit playing." Chris slowly pulled off Tomorrow's dress.

He admired her body like it was sculptured art. Once he had Tomorrow completely naked, he stripped down as well. Tomorrow gazed at his amazing physique and couldn't wait until their bodies were touching. She was finally ready to experience Chris on a whole new level.

He softly nibbled on her feet before making his way up to the rest of her body. He placed soft kisses on her legs and in between her thighs. He finally made his way to her breasts and slowly tickled his tongue over her erect nipples. Tomorrow moaned softly in delight.

Chris was so gentle with her, but she yearned to feel him deep inside of her. She felt a sense of urgency, but he continued to take his time.

"Sit up," Chris demanded.

"Huh?" Tomorrow was knocked out of her trance. She was in complete pleasure and all of a sudden, it had ended.

"I wanna share something with you. I ain't never tried it, but I read up on it," Chris explained.

Tomorrow hoped that Chris wasn't up to trying any overly freaky activities. She was rather adventurous herself, but there were just some places she would not go.

If this nigga tries to piss on me or stick his dick in my ass, I may have to kill him.

"Get that look off your face. It ain't nothing crazy." Chris chuckled.

"Just checking, you know how niggas try and get creative."

"Here, get a little closer and sit Indian style. Now straddle my lap," Chris instructed.

"This is called the Yab-Yom position."

"The who?"

"Yab-Yom." Chris grinned.

"Take my hands. I want you to take a deep inhale when I exhale and then you exhale once I inhale," he continued.

"Should I close my eyes and chant or something?" Tomorrow joked.

"No. Keep your eyes opened. I wanna see you and I want you to see me. But you can't laugh or talk. We have to be serious in order for it to work."

"Okay," Tomorrow replied.

She did as instructed and Chris did the same. They inhaled each other's breath using the Tantric practices that Chris showed her. There was an ultimate release and a strong sense of eroticism swept through them. But this was different; it wasn't just a normal erotic feeling, this was exotic and exciting.

They felt as though they were climaxing before any penetration had taken place.

"Mmmm," Tomorrow moaned aloud.

"Damn. You felt that too, huh?" Chris laughed.

"Yeah. What the hell you just do to me?"

"It's called Tantra. It's like a higher level of intimacy and it's supposed to make the orgasm so much better. I wanted to experience that with you. I told you, you're special to me."

The two just stared at each other for a few moments, intensifying their urges to become one. Their gazes were so deep that it was as if they were both hypnotized.

"This shit is scary. I can't control what I'm feeling," Tomorrow whispered.

"So don't." Chris leaned in and kissed her.

Tomorrow moaned in delight when Chris finally inserted all ten inches of pure chocolate bliss deep inside of her. His touch sent chills throughout her entire body and his slow and powerful long stroke had her legs shaking uncontrollably.

Soft splatters of her pussy juice made its way to Chris' dick and caused him to go deeper. He loved the feeling of her wetness dripping from him and the harder he stroked, the wetter she became.

Chris found himself moaning as well. Her pussy pulsated around his dick creating an even tighter fit. It was as if they were made especially to please each other.

"Damn. This shit right here..." Chris couldn't even finish his statement. He closed his eyes and sped up the pace just enough to hear Tomorrow's high pitched moan.

"Yes. Just like that!" Tomorrow screamed.

Before they knew it, they had created their own little kama sutra. Tomorrow managed to twist into positions that she never thought she could get into. Chris had her completely open and she was enjoying every second of it.

By the end of the night, they were completely covered in each other's love juice and exhausted from the hours of lovemaking.

Tomorrow had a real smile on her face for the first time in a long time. The entire night, she waited for the urge to kill, but it never came. Not that she was looking for it, but since it had been occurring for months, she just expected it to show up. To her surprise, the impulse was nowhere in sight.

She knew that Chris had to be the one and hoped for his sake that he wasn't just trying to play her.

Tomorrow laid her head on Chris' chest. He playfully wrapped one of her locs around his pointer finger and exhaled.

"Did you mean what you said about always being there?" Tomorrow asked while tracing her fingers up and down his chiseled chest.

"Always, shawty. I love you, Tomorrow," Chris said without hesitation.

"I love you too."

***

Tomorrow's phone rang and she almost didn't want to get up. She and Chris had shared such a wonderful night together that she didn't want to ruin it with a phone call.

Who the hell is calling at 3 a.m.?

"Hello?"

"Yeah, bitch. You thought you killed a nigga, but I ain't dead and when I catch up to you, I'mma finish fucking you, then I'mma slit your throat."

Tomorrow rushed into the bathroom to finish the call. She didn't want Chris to hear anything that was said. He still didn't know everything about her.

"Nigga, I'm obviously not afraid of you," Tomorrow whispered.

"Bitch, I ain't finish what I started, but believe I will. You're dead, bitch."

"If you call my phone again, I will personally take a trip up to the hospital and remove your rectum," Tomorrow threatened.

"Oh, you ain't hear, bitch? I'm being released. Next week. And believe once I'm fully healed, it won't be shit that can stop me from gunning for you. You fucked with the wrong nigga."

"Well, I guess it's a date. Later."

Tomorrow hung up the phone. There was always something that stood in the way of her true happiness. She couldn't even enjoy one peaceful night without being threatened by a guy who should've been dead. She knew that before long, she would have some major drama on her hands.

She assumed that being with Chris would solve all the problems in the world, but what she didn't know was that it would only get worse from here.

CHAPTER

~ 18 ~

"Ahh fuck! Everybody shut the fuck up! Yo Rico, put the gun back in that nigga's mouth! Chris, go check out the window for them boyz, shit, you know we in VA".

The room became silent while Brandon answered his cell phone.

"Hey beautiful, did you get the room yet?"

"Just checked in. When you coming? I'm wearing that red lingerie outfit you bought me from Ocean City."

"Ahh shit, baby, I'm gonna be at least another hour or so. Look, I'mma call you when I get on the road. Did you eat?"

"Nah, can you pick me up some chicken wings? And don't forget to ask for extra mumbo sauce this time."

"A'right cool, see you in a few. Don't take that outfit off either! Shit, a nigga horny as fuck, trying to eat sum pussy tonight."

"Mmm, that's what I'm talkin' 'bout. I'll see you soon, boo."

"Aight, gone."

Brandon put his phone back in his hoodie and continued his prior conversation.

"So Mike, you smokin' my shit?" He asked calmly with his arms folded.

Rico took the gun out of Mike's mouth and allowed him to speak. He held it at the side of Mike's head, just waiting for the okay to pull the trigger.

"Brandon look, I told you I will have your money. Just give me a week, that's all I need! Nigga, please!" Mike begged.

"Answer the muthafuckin' question. Are you smokin' my shit?!"

Brandon slammed his fist down on Mike's dining room table and glared at him with a deadly stare.

Mike grew nervous. He quickly fell to his knees and begged for mercy.

"Come on, you know I'm good for it. Times been hard, man. Nigga can't find a job, my woman constantly on my back naggin'. Just give me a little more time, that's all I need!"

"That's why I let you get on the team in the first place, you punk ass bitch! I already know your backstory! I let you hold a lil' sumthin' to sell, not smoke! Now how much money did you make on the block? I know Alexandria is full of thirsty crackheads!"

Mike put his head down in shame. He had made a little money, but not the amount that Brandon was expecting. Chris and Rico pulled him back onto the chair.

"I got about $1,100 in my pocket. But I swear I will

198

have the rest."

Brandon's face grew angrier. He couldn't believe that Mike had the audacity to try and shortchange him.

"Nigga, I gave you $4,500 worth of shit, and you smoked all but $1,100 of it?" Brandon screamed.

"Ahh, come on, what am I gonna do? Run? Brandon, you're like a son to me. You're sleeping with my stepdaughter for Christ sake!" Mike sobbed.

Everyone laughed at Mike's expense.

"She ain't your damn stepdaughter, nigga! You and Flo ain't even married. I been knowing Mishon's ass for like seven years now, waaay before she met my cuz Brandon, and she ain't neva had nuthin' nice to say about yo' ass!" Rico chimed in.

"Yeah, she be tellin' me how you be up in here flexin' on her. Fake acting like you the man of the house and shit! Baby girl can't even sleep in her own crib cuz of yo' lazy ass!" Brandon added.

"Hey Brandon, no disrespect, but how this house is ran is decided between me and Flo. Mishon and I butt heads because she has no respect for me and the—"

"Would you like to know why she don't respect you?" Brandon politely interrupted.

Brandon scooted his chair closer to Mike. Rico took his gun away from Mike's head.

"Because you're weak," Brandon softly answered. "Nigga, look at you! You're damn near forty-something years old, and what you got to show for it, nigga? Nuthin'! And you claim to be the man of the house? Your priorities is all fucked up."

Brandon pointed his finger directly in Mike's face.

"I might as well be Mishon's daddy. I do more for her than you do for her or her mother. Do you really think I would have my bitch working all day and night? But I bet you cash dem bi-weekly checks, huh? Instead of standing on your own two feet, you stand on your bitch's back. Now you want to cry like a lil' bitch when times get rough? That's what men do,they make a way outta no muthafuckin' way. You ain't no real ass nigga. You's a waste! You ain't even worth the flesh God allowed you to rent. You a garbage ass nigga!"

Mike began to cry and allowed the tears to roll down his face. He was at a loss for words. A twenty-year-old had just insulted his manhood and there was nothing he could say or do about it. But Brandon wasn't finished.

"I took Mishon under my wing cuz she was yearnin' for love. Her daddy broke on her when she was little, and the only parent she has left is pulling overtime to look after yo' sorry ass! I love her to death. She's a muthafuckin' ride or die, but I guess you wouldn't know shit about that! You ain't got loyalty to nobody out here. You in it for your damn self. But I'll tell you this much, your days are numbered, nigga, and I swear to fucking God, If you ever flex on her like that again, I will go find your mother and shoot her in the fucking head for even creating a fucking tragedy like you!"

Mike knew that Brandon was telling the truth. He had been a sorry excuse for a boyfriend and a stepfather, but he didn't want to die because of it. He promised himself that if he made it out of this situation alive, he was going to rehab.

"Now back to the situation at hand, you mark ass bitch! I want my fucking money! I wish these niggas stop trying me out here. They just don't fucking get it, do they? Don't fuck with me! I'mma ill ass nigga, I don't have time for these games. Nigga, what you think this is, the United Negro College Fund, muthafucka? I'm not a charitable ass nigga! Even my mama pay for every rock she smoke, nigga! No freebies over here, so don't run that whole family shit by me, cuz I ain't even tryna hear that shit!"

Brandon flipped over Mike's table and caused the glass top to shatter. Chris grabbed Brandon from behind and held him back. He knew that when Brandon was upset, all bets were officially off. Brandon was generally a calm dude, but yet again, someone had tried to get over and he simply wasn't having it.

Chris knew that any more time spent in that house would lead to bloodshed, and now just wasn't the right time. They had to get out of there before shit got real.

Rico ran into the back and ransacked Mike's entire bedroom. He hoped to find more money or even some jewelry to take as collateral.

"Yo look, this nigga got a rolex!" Rico said.

He tried on the watch and showed it off to Chris and Brandon.

"Hmph, that nigga ain't buy shit! Flo bought his broke ass that watch, but we gonna see what we can get for it on the street," Brandon said, staring dead into Mike's eyes.

"Yep, you can get at least a G on the block for it," Chris added.

Brandon walked up to Mike and spit in his face. Normally that wasn't his style, but Brandon despised Mike as much as Mishon did. He tried to have some respect for him, but now that he was interfering with business, it was a done deal.

Mike looked so pathetic sitting there in the chair. Brandon decided to give him the benefit of the doubt. He was going to allow some time for him to come up with the money, but if he failed, Mike would definitely get some fresh bullets up in him.

"Nigga, I'mma give you a week to have my bread. If you don't have it, it will be lights out for that ass, understood?"

Mike shook his head up and down.

"Let's go," Brandon said to Rico and Chris before they

ran outta Mike's place in a rush.

Mike sat still and waited for Brandon and his goons to leave before he got up out the chair. He ran to the door and locked it. He knew that he had no choice but to make a phone call to the person who owed him the most.

"Hello?"

"Yeah, Tomorrow. It's me, Mike. Look, I need a huge favor!"

"What!?"

"I kinda got hemmed up today. I need to hold some money."

"Nigga, I ain't givin' you shit! What the fuck you think this is?"

"Look, I helped you out! I took care of that nigga for you and got that video back!"

"Ummm, thanks, but what's your point? I paid you $500 for that job, and you got some good pussy outta the deal too!"

"Well, when that tape magically resurfaces, then what you gonna do?"

"Oh, so it's like that now? That's fine. Nigga, how much you need?"

"About $3,400. Look, I'mma pay you back, T, I just got in a bind, that's all."

"You gonna have to do a lil' sumthing for me to let go of that type of money."

"Like what?!"

"You gonna have to be eating my pussy for breakfast, lunch and dinner, nigga. Hmph!"

"That's sounds delicious. You know Flo gone? She won't be back until tomorrow night. Yeah, come to daddy so I can suck the shit out of that clit. I knew you would come to your senses, baby."

"Yeah, okay. I will be over there in an hour."

Mike hung up the phone and pulled a little bag full of crack rocks from his Timbs. He then pulled out his pipe and smoked until his mind was free of all his problems. Once his high had reached its peek, he decided that he needed to go clean up. He turned on his shower and removed his jeans that were covered in piss.

Mike shook his head at the fact that he had allowed those young dudes to have him that afraid. He was losing control of his life and dope was the cause of it all.

He jumped in the steaming shower and sighed. He was so happy that Tomorrow had agreed to give him the money. He knew that she was due to arrive soon, and he would have to be on point.

He smiled knowing that all of his troubles had been solved, at least for now.

CHAPTER

~ 19 ~

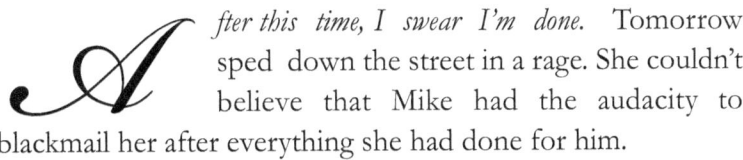*fter this time, I swear I'm done.* Tomorrow sped down the street in a rage. She couldn't believe that Mike had the audacity to blackmail her after everything she had done for him.

Mike was Mishon's so-called "stepfather," and even though he was fine, initially he was off limits. Not only was she half his age, but he was a lazy dope fiend that lived off of his woman. But that didn't keep him from eyeing Tomorrow.

Every time Tomorrow would come over and visit Mishon, she noticed that Mike would always give her compliments and make slick comments whenever Mishon wasn't watching. She thought he was bold as hell to even attempt something like that, but was intrigued to find out if he could back up his propositions.

Tomorrow had gone way too far with Mike, and the only reason she hadn't killed him thus far was because they had built a special bond over the years. He was her first and had shown her things that ultimately helped shape her into the seductress she had become, and for that, she felt like she owed him something.

But the fact still remained that he was her best friend's stepdad. Even though Mishon couldn't stand him, she knew that there could be major repercussions to anyone ever finding out about their history.

But tonight was different. Mike had to die. He simply knew too much. It was time for Tomorrow to cover up all her loose ends so that she could get the proper help that she needed and finally live happily with Chris. She didn't want any more secrets between them, especially not ones that could come back and bite her in the ass. After all this was over, she would sit down with Chris and have a long talk. Hopefully, he would understand her past indiscretions, or at least be accepting.

Tomorrow slid on her Versace shades, put on a fresh coat of Tom Ford Scarlet Rouge lipstick and wrapped her locs into a bun. She grabbed her Prada duffel bag from the back seat and gave herself one final glance in her rearview mirror.

She stepped out of her BMW wearing nothing but a sexy black trench coat and four-inch black Manolo Blahnik leather pumps. She was dressed to kill. She strutted her way up to Mike's apartment and knocked on the door.

When he answered, his face read that he was rather excited to see her. Not only was he going to dodge a bullet by getting this money, he was about to have fun doing it.

Tomorrow walked right past him without saying a word. She entered the apartment and headed straight for his bedroom.

"I have something for you," Tomorrow said, breaking

the silence.

"Oh, daddy has something for you too, baby," Mike said flirtatiously.

Tomorrow slowly opened her trench coat and revealed her naked body. She was covered in honey and had a white residue clinging from her breast that trailed down her stomach and made its way down to her lovely pearl. Mike's eyes grew wide when he realized what it was.

"Is that what I think it is?" Mike got closer.

He took his index finger and slid it across her left breast allowing the residue to get onto his fingers. Mike tasted his finger and his mouth immediately went numb.

"Pure cocaine, baby." Tomorrow giggled.

Mike stood there for a moment unable to speak. He couldn't believe that Tomorrow had come to his house covered in cocaine. He wondered how she even knew that he was into drugs.

"What's wrong, baby? You look like you seen a ghost. Isn't this the real reason you want me here anyway?" Tomorrow grabbed Mike's finger and trailed it down her body. There's more where that came from."

Tomorrow went over to her duffel bag and retrieved another bag from it. She poured the bag's contents all over Mike's bed. His eyes widened when he saw several stacks of cash and bags of dope spread all over his bed. She climbed into the center of the bed and laid flat on her back.

"C'mon, daddy. Lick all of this off me so we can really get the party started."

Mike couldn't fight the urge. He rushed over to his bed and began licking every spot on Tomorrow's body that held the coke residue.

He traced her nipples with his tongue and finger fucked her pussy simultaneously. He sucked each of his fingers ingesting a tasty combination of cocaine, honey and pussy juice.

"I wanna try something different with you. Will you allow me to do that?" Tomorrow questioned as Mike deliciously devoured her pussy.

He lifted his head up from her twat, sporting a white ring around his mouth and Tomorrow's glaze on his chin.

"Sure, baby. What did you have in mind?"

Tomorrow jumped up and headed towards the kitchen. Mike sat on the edge of the bed and anxiously awaited Tomorrow's return. A few seconds later, she returned to the room with a chair in hand and sat it across from the bed.

"What's that for?" Mike asked impatiently.

"For you of course, baby. I wanna play victim and sexy psycho killer," Tomorrow enticingly said.

"Damn, T, you know how I like this freaky shit!" Mike got excited and ran over and sat in the chair.

"This is gonna be easier than I thought." Tomorrow laughed to herself.

She went over to her duffel bag and pulled out a rope. She bound Mike by his hands and feet and made sure he was strapped securely to the chair.

"What's the safe word?" Mike inquired.

"Crackhead," She whispered in Mike's ear.

"What?" He asked confused.

"You heard me, crackhead." Tomorrow giggled.

He didn't like hearing Tomorrow call him names, but he decided to just play along.

"Please don't kill me, sexy psycho killer," Mike begged.

"Shut the fuck up," Tomorrow demanded.

Tomorrow abruptly left the room and headed down the hallway. She wanted her final murder to be something special. She rummaged through the kitchen and found a sharp metal cheese grater.

"Perfect," she said to herself.

She could hear Mike yelling from the room. The fact that he allowed her to tie him up willingly made her chuckle to herself.

Tomorrow walked back down the hall and entered the room with the cheese grater in hand.

"I told you to shut the fuck up, didn't I?" Tomorrow said angrily.

"Yes, sexy psycho killer. I'm so sorry, please don't kill me." Mike pretended to cry.

"Where'd you put the video tape?"

"In a black Adidas gym bag under the bed. Now that you have it, please, please don't kill me."

"Sorry, unfortunately I can't promise you that." Tomorrow laughed.

She dropped down on all fours and crawled over to the bed. She found the Adidas bag exactly where Mike said it would be and removed the video tape. Tomorrow immediately destroyed the video and placed it inside of her duffel bag. She pulled out a pair of her thongs and walked back over to Mike.

"Well, can you at least grant my dying wish and fuck the shit outta me?" Mike laughed, trying his best to stay in character.

"Usually I would, but unfortunately, this is business," Tomorrow said dryly.

She picked up the cheese grater that now sat next to Mike. He wondered what kind of kinky things she had planned for him with that. It didn't look like it could be that fun, but he was open to trying anything once.

"Please, sexy psycho killer. Lemme just get a taste of that sweet pussy one last time," Mike begged.

"I really like you, Mike. I let you live because I really liked you. Good dick, very sexy and kinky just like me, and we've been through so much. Oh but no, you had to go and mess it up, huh?"

Mike stopped begging. He was beginning to think that maybe this wasn't a game. Tomorrow was getting a little too serious for his own taste.

"Huh?"

"You really thought I was gonna just give you my money, you fucking crackhead?" Tomorrow screamed. "You thought I was gonna allow you to blackmail me and not get back at your ass?"

"T, what are you doing? We supposed to be role playing, baby," Mike shrieked.

"I told you to shut the fuck up!"

Tomorrow slid the cheese grater across Mike's left knee and he screamed in pain.

"Ahh, what the fuck is wrong with you?"

"I'm the sexy psycho killer, remember?" Tomorrow smiled and grated his right knee.

"Ouch, bitch!" Mike screamed.

"That's Kiss of Death to you, muthafucka."

"That's you?" Mike questioned.

"Yep. Check the lipstick, nigga. Muah!" Tomorrow giggled and puckered up.

Tomorrow picked up the pace and began grating Mike's knees like he was shredded cheese. She watched in delight as both of Mike's knees started to bleed uncontrollably. The harder she grated his knees, the louder he got. She took her thong and stuffed it into his mouth to lessen his screams.

He began to sob and begged Tomorrow to let him go.

"Ah, Ah, Ahhhh. You have to say the safe word first!" Tomorrow taunted.

Mike shook his head "no."

"Oh yes. C'mon, you can do it. Say the safe word,

Mike."

Tomorrow took the grater and went across both of Mike's knees even harder. She removed the thong from his mouth to give him one last chance to say it.

"Go ahead. Say it. Say what the fuck you are!" Tomorrow demanded.

Mike sobbed even harder. How had he gotten himself into this mess? Had he just stayed on the straight and narrow and treated Flo with some respect, he wouldn't even be dealing with the unnecessary drama.

"A crackhead," Mike muttered under his breath.

"I can't heeeeeear you, Mike. Say it louder. Say it like you're proud to be a fucking head!" Tomorrow laughed.

Mike cried even more.

"Don't cry now, nigga. You should've cried when you started wasting your punk ass life away on the rocks. You see why they say drugs are bad? There's no hope in dope and allat other shit. Nigga, did you fall asleep at the D.A.R.E. program?" Tomorrow joked.

"T, please don't do this. Let's talk about this. We can work it out. I was gonna give the money right back. I swear," Mike pleaded.

"Too late. You tried to blackmail me, and now I can't trust you. I wish things could be different because you had great dick, but that's all over now."

"Please, T."

"You still haven't repeated the safe word. Say it and I'll let you go. Scream it to the top of the fucking world, Mike!" Tomorrow screamed.

"*CRACKHEAD.* I'm a fucking crackhead!" Mike cried.

Tomorrow laughed at Mike's tears.

"Good job, Mike. You know what I'mma do for you? I'm gonna take you outta your misery. I was gonna let you go, but I had a better thought. Why not just kill you. You're gonna die eventually anyway with all that crack and dope that you shoot into your system."

"Crackhead, crackhead, crackead!" Mike screamed the safe word.

"Too late, nigga. Game over."

Tomorrow walked over to her duffel bag and pulled out Dexter. Mike's eyes grew wide as she inched towards him. She stabbed Mike in the throat with the knife and sighed.

Damn. That was hard.

She leaned over and placed the final kiss on Mike's forehead. She allowed the kiss to linger for awhile because she actually had deep feelings for Mike. He had been more than just some random dude she killed. They had history.

Tomorrow had never killed someone so close to her, and the emotional feelings behind it were oh so real. She had to get the fuck out of there before she started to get sloppy.

Tomorrow placed Dexter back into her duffel bag. She slid her trench coat back on, and after a quick clean up, she gathered everything that could link her to the murder and headed out of the door in a rush.

She walked down the hall and heard what sounded like a camera flashing. Tomorrow turned to see Legacy standing before her with a deviant smile on her face. She had followed Tomorrow and was planning a little blackmail of her own.

"Say cheese, bitch!" Legacy yelled.

She waved her camera in front of Tomorrow's face. Legacy finally had what she needed to make Tomorrow disappear.

Tomorrow had to give it to her, she definitely hadn't seen this one coming, but she refused to go down without a fight. If Legacy wanted to be in the big leagues, Tomorrow was going to show her exactly how it was done.

"Let's take a ride. We have some shit we need to discuss," Legacy sneered.

"Oh yes, we definitely do." Tomorrow smiled.

Tomorrow clicked the automatic door lock and allowed Legacy to open the passenger door to her car. There was silence between the two, and neither wanted to start off the conversation.

Deep inside, Legacy was nervous because she had never confronted anyone at this capacity, but she was excited because she had finally done something right.

Tomorrow could see the nervousness in Legacy's expression. The tenseness showed on Legacy's face as she slid into the passenger seat with her camera in hand.

Tomorrow just smiled. She knew that there was no way she'd allow Legacy to keep those photos. She already knew what Legacy had planned for her, but she hadn't expected to have to deal with it so soon.

She grabbed her duffel bag from the back seat and slid off her trench coat. Legacy watched as Tomorrow nakedly pulled out a pair of bra and panties.

What kinda freaky shit was that bitch doing in there? Legacy thought.

Tomorrow went back into the bag and pulled out a pink maxi dress and slipped it over her head. She knew that Legacy was watching her, so she played it cool. Her plan was to be as nonchalant as possible. She'd never let Legacy see her sweat.

"So," Tomorrow began once she had everything in order. "To what do I owe the pleasure of this meeting Legacy?"

"Cut the bullshit, bitch. Why the fuck are you stepping out of Mishon's house when she and Flo ain't even home?" Legacy questioned. "And yo' ass is butt ass naked under a fuckin' trench coat!" she squealed.

213

She had Tomorrow right where she wanted her. Now that she had the information she needed, she planned to reveal it all to Mishon. She knew that there was no way Mishon would still be friends with Tomorrow once she knew that she was sleeping with Mike.

"It's funny that you ask that. I had to handle some business," Tomorrow replied cheerfully.

Tomorrow put the car in drive and headed towards Interstate 495. She had a special little plan of her own for Legacy. Killing her traditionally would never work. Tomorrow knew that there was a chance that they had been spotted together, so her plan had to be untraceable.

"What kinda business could you possibly have with Mike? Unless you fucking him like you were fucking Kane, bitch!" Legacy replied, answering her own question.

"You act like such an uppity and perfect bitch, but you ain't nothing but a scandalous, grimy ass ho who only gives a fuck about herself," she declared.

Tomorrow just laughed. What could she really say? All of those things were indeed true.

"Buuuusted." Tomorrow giggled.

"Bitch, you really think this shit is funny? Ruining people's lives ain't fuckin' funny, bitch. But you know what the fuck is funny?" Legacy screamed.

"Enlighten me," Tomorrow sneered.

"It's gon' be mighty fucking funny when I let everybody know who the real muthafuckin' Tomorrow Robinson is. Bitch, I found your medicine and I know your ass is bipolar," Legacy declared.

"Damn. You got me. It's true." Tomorrow pretended to be shocked.

"Yeah, bitch, I've been following your ass around. I wonder what the fuck Chris is gonna say once he knows your bipolar ass has been kicking it with other niggas since you been back from Ocean City. Yeah, that's right, bitch. I been following yo' ass, and now you caught the fuck up!"

Tomorrow's face immediately switched from nice and sweet to dark and perverse. She took her eyes off the road and her head quickly snapped in Legacy's direction.

Legacy had just said the wrong thing. It was one thing to blackmail Tomorrow, but playing around with her only chance at true love was an automatic trigger to kill.

Hearing Chris' name sent Tomorrow into a frenzy. She tightly clutched her steering wheel and began to accelerate the car's speed.

"You wanna know what I was doing in that apartment, Legacy?"

Tomorrow's breathing became constant and heavy. Legacy stared at her as if she had just realized that perhaps she was fucking with the wrong person.

"I was in there grating Mike's mutherfucking kneecaps. He's dead. And you wanna know why he's dead?" Tomorrow screamed.

"Because he couldn't mind his own fuckin' business. Like you, he wanted to blackmail me. He wanted to destroy me and tarnish my fuckin' image. Do you honestly think I'mma let that shit happen, bitch?"

Tomorrow was now driving at full speed. The car was racing down the highway at nearly 100 miles per hour. Legacy's eyes grew wide and she held on tightly to her seat, grabbing it for dear life.

"Slow the fuck down! What the fuck are you doing, you crazy bitch?! Pull this car over now!" Legacy screamed.

"No, bitch. You wanna stomp with the muthafuckin' big dogs, huh? I'll kill both of our asses in this bitch!" Tomorrow screamed even louder.

She noticed Legacy gasping for air. A smile spread across Tomorrow's face. She rolled down the windows and allowed the breeze to engulf the car.

Legacy was in the full process of having an asthma attack. She watched as Legacy grabbed for her purse and pulled out the small red inhaler. But there was no way Tomorrow was going to allow her to use it.

Legacy fumbled with the inhaler and struggled to put it up to her mouth. Tomorrow snatched the inhaler and threw it out of the window. They both heard the inhaler clink against the car and shatter on the highway pavement.

"You bi—bitch!" Legacy struggled to say.

"What's wrong, Legacy? Are you having an asthma attack? You can't breathe? Here, enjoy some of the air. Stick your head out the window," Tomorrow taunted as she rolled down Legacy's window a little more.

Legacy could feel herself getting lightheaded. She knew if she didn't get to a hospital soon, it would all be over. Her life flashed before her eyes and she wondered if all this back and forth with Tomorrow had really been worth it. She fought to hold on to her final breaths, not wanting to lose to Tomorrow yet again.

Tomorrow slowed down the speed of the car. She slipped on her Versace shades and started cruising down the highway. She headed in the direction of Virginia Medical Center.

"I'm not sure what appropriate death music is, but you like Beyonce, right?" Tomorrow laughed.

She turned Beyonce's "Freakum Dress" on full blast so that she wouldn't have to hear the annoying sounds of Legacy's death. Tomorrow danced in her seat and purposely sang off key.

After a few moments, she looked over and noticed

Legacy was slumped over.

"Damn, son." Tomorrow shook her head.

Frantically, she pulled out her cell phone and called 911.

"911, what is your emergency?"

"My best friend is having an asthma attack and I don't know what to do. She doesn't have her inhaler!" Tomorrow screamed.

"Just calm down. You need to get your friend to the hospital immediately."

"I'm headed there now! Can you stay on the phone with me?" Tomorrow cried.

"Yes. What's your name? I'm Nancy."

"Tomorrow!"

"Okay, Tomorrow, you have to stay calm. Is your friend responsive?"

"She's blacking out, it does—it doesn't look good!" Tomorrow screamed.

After a few minutes, Tomorrow arrived at the hospital and jumped out of the car.

"Somebody please! Anyone please help!" She screamed with tears streaming down her face.

The medics rushed to the car and pulled out Legacy's dead body. They told Tomorrow to sit and wait in the lobby. She overheard one of them say "Yeah this one is a D.O.A. go ahead and call it."

Tomorrow put her head down into her lap and pretended to cry.

She laughed hysterically at the thought that she had just gotten away with the perfect murder.

Okay, I'm done for real this time.

CHAPTER

~ 20 ~

"Mishon, wake up! Wake up!"

"What, Brandon, shit!"

"Yo, your phone has been ringing off the hook. Answer that shit. It's like eight in the morning."

Mishon rolled over and grabbed her phone from the nightstand. She was blinded by the early morning sunlight that peered through the window and she couldn't make out the name on the caller ID.

"Hellooo?" Mishon said in an annoyed tone.

"Shon? Shon? Can you hear me!?"

"Mom? Wait, slow down. What's wrong?"

Mishon sat up in the bed and stretched out her arms. She hadn't heard from her mother in weeks, and now she was calling with some crazy gossip? It was simply too early in the morning for her to be dealing with this mess.

"Where are you, Shon?" Flo sounded concerned.

"I'm with Brandon, why? Mom, what the fuck is goin' on?"

"You stay away from that no good ass nigga! He ain't no fucking good! He's a murderer!"

Mishon listened. She shook Brandon repeatedly, attempting to wake him from his deep sleep. He rolled over and glared at Mishon with a look of disdain, but when he noticed her facial expression change from annoyed to concerned, he immediately sat up and listened in on the conversation.

"What?" Mishon screamed.

"Mike's dead! It was awful! I found him this morning when I came home from work. The apartment manager reviewed the tapes and caught Brandon on surveillance walking out of the building last night with a few other people! Ugh, just turn on the fucking news!" Flo cried.

Brandon snatched the phone out of Mishon's hand and ended the call. They looked each other in the eyes for a few moments trying to wrap their minds around what had just happened.

"Brandon, what's going on?"

Brandon ignored Mishon and turned on the TV. He could feel the newfound tension in the room. He sat at the edge of the bed to avoid conflict with Mishon.

"Brandon!" Mishon said with a firm tone.

"Not now, Mishon! Let me figure out what the fuck is goin' on first before you start drilling me and shit!"

Brandon stood up and picked his pants up off the floor. He dug into his pockets to find his phone. When he finally retrieved it, he realized it was dead.

"Shon, let me get your charger for a sec. Fuck man! What's up with all these damn commercials?" Brandon flipped the channels frantically hoping to find the news.

Mishon scrambled to get her charger for Brandon. She noticed Brandon's expression. He was ready to snap at any moment. She decided that she would stay silent, at least until the news came on and they figured out what was really going on.

"Here."

Brandon took the charger and plugged it into the wall. He powered his phone up and waited until it was fully updated. He immediately checked his voicemail.

"Damn, I got like thirteen voicemails."

All of Brandon's voicemails were from Rico and he sounded extremely frantic.

"Yo Brandon, shit just got real as fuck. Wherever you at, just stay there and lay low for a while. Nigga, hit me as soon as you get this!"

Mishon and Brandon continued to flip through the channels until they finally found a news station discussing the murder. They both paid close attention.

"We're back and trailing a story in Alexandria this morning where authorities believe that the Lipstick Serial Killer, known to most as the Kiss of Death, might have struck again! But this time, she may not have acted alone.

A 46 year old male named Mike Watson was discovered dead in his condo this morning by his girlfriend. He was found strapped to a chair and tortured to death with what appears to be a cheese grater, sealed with a lipstick kiss on his forehead. But a stab wound to the neck was what ultimately killed him.

Highpoint Condominiums' manager Robert Cunningham released a surveillance tape to authorities showing three suspicious people entering through the lobby and riding the elevator up to Watson's apartment, but only person could be seen clearly enough for Watson's girlfriend to make a positive ID.

Police are now looking for Brandon James, the boyfriend of the victim's stepdaughter.

If anyone knows his whereabouts, please call the Alexandria Police Department. Right now, he is only wanted for questioning in this murder."

Brandon turned the TV off and threw the remote, hitting the wall just above the television.

"Baby girl, I swear to you I didn't kill that nigga. I swear on everything I didn't."

"Why were you even there? Who were those other people you were wit'?"

"All you need to know is that me and my peoples went over there to handle that nigga. He tried to run up on me at the store and he had to be dealt wit! But I ain't kill that nigga! Do you really think that I would do a sloppy ass job like that? C'mon, Mishon, think about it. A fucking cheese grater and a kiss on the forehead! Nah, that ain't my work! I would've been put two bullets in that nigga's head and called it a fucking day!"

"So when I called you last night and you were talking about how you were handling business, you were really there?"

"Yeah." Brandon sighed.

Mishon sat on the edge of the bed and straddled Brandon. She believed in her heart that Brandon wouldn't do something so foul. She kissed him on the forehead and then immediately jumped up.

"Oh my God, Brandon!"

"What?"

"The kiss! The kiss on the forehead!"

"Yeah, what about it? I didn't do that shit."

"I know, but clearly somebody set you up. They wanted it to look like a Kiss of Death murder, but you probably got in the way. I mean, think about it. Somebody must've seen you and your goons comin' out the building then went upstairs to make a move."

"But still, why would the cops want to talk to me then?"

"Brandon, you were the last person seen there. Maybe they just want to question you. Who knows."

Brandon sat in silence thinking about what Mishon had said. He didn't want to get locked up, especially not in Virginia.

"So what you think I should do then?" Brandon asked.

"I think you should turn yourself in so it doesn't look like you on the run."

"Nah, fuck that, Mishon! I ain't going to jail! Not in VA Hell nah!"

Mishon's cell phone rang. It was a number she didn't recognize. She shot Brandon a confused look and then finally answered the call.

"Yes, hello?"

"Mishon, this is Chief Doug Allenham from the Alexandria Police Department. Now I want you to listen carefully."

"I'm listening."

"Your mother, Ms. Florentine Copeland, is here at the station. She informed me that you are with Brandon Jackson, correct?"

"Did she? Nah, Brandon left about an hour ago."

"Left from where?"

"Just know he left and that's all I got to say. Goodbye!"

"Wait, Mishon, I know you're with him. He's probably standing right there next to you as we speak. I must assure you that you can be charged with obstruction of justice if we find out that you know where he is. All we want to do is talk to him, that's all. If he continues to run, he could potentially face serious charges."

"Look, I told you I ain't wit' that nigga and that's the last muthafucking time I'mma tell you! Tell my mother to eat a dick and mind her fucking business!"

Mishon hung up the phone. She was nervous and it read all over her face. How had this happened? Why was Brandon even anywhere near Mike? Too many thoughts ran through her head at once. What was she going to do?

"Who was that on the phone, Mishon?" Brandon yelled and snapped her back into reality.

"It was the Alexandria Police Department, they know we're together. My mother is down at the station."

"Fuck it! Just take me to the damn station. They ain't got shit on me and I know I ain't kill that punk ass nigga. Whatever happens, happens."

Brandon and Mishon quickly got dressed and packed up their things.

"Look, I want you to follow me to my crib so I can park my car. Then I'mma need you to call Rico and tell him to look after my mom, cuz shit, ain't no tellin' how long I'mma be gone."

"It's just questioning, Brandon. You just gon' go in and talk to them niggas and come right back out."

"Don't be stupid. You know who we fucking with right now? This is some serious shit. They don't say your name on TV unless some shit really bout to go down, Shon. They think this shit is in connection to the Kiss of Death, a bitch who been on a killing rampage. They gon' do a little more than just talking, trust me!" Brandon yelled.

He kicked over his Adidas bag and knocked his clothes to the floor. Brandon couldn't believe this was happening. He knew he had to get a grip because one slightest hint of weakness, and he would be going down for a murder he didn't commit. He knew he had to get it together. His people were depending on him.

"Listen, I'm sorry, baby. It's just too much shit going on right now," he continued. "I need you to just do what I asked, okay?"

"Okay." Mishon cried as she continued gathering her things.

Brandon pulled out a roll of $100 bills and tossed it to her.

"Look, everything is going to be okay. Here, take this money. There should be about $3,000 there. Oh, and hold on to my wallet. You know I get my trust fund money every month. That should take care of all the utilities at my house. Make sure you take my debit card and pay 'em."

Mishon nodded, letting Brandon know that she had everything under control. She always knew that with Brandon's lifestyle as a drug dealer, there was a chance that a day like this would come. She just didn't expect it to come so soon, and definitely not in this way.

She knew she had to be his ride or die, and that's exactly what she was going to do.

She wiped her tears and grabbed her bags from the bed.

"You ready to go?"

"Yeah, let me grab my keys."

Mishon met up with her friends at the Table Talk. She broke down in tears as she tried to explain what had taken place earlier that morning.

"I don't know what to do. Everything was such a blur. And after all this shit, I can't believe my mom threw me out the house." Mishon wiped her face.

"Don't even trip off that shit. You know you more than welcome to stay over Brandon's house. Shit, to be honest, he wanted you to live there anyway so you wouldn't have to feel threatened all the damn time like you did at home. So you know you good. We got you. Just let me know, and me and my niggas will come move your shit," Rico assured her.

"Okay."

"Don't worry, I got Brandon the best lawyer in the DMV," Chris said. "He should be at the jail by now. I told him everything that he needed to know about the case, and he said that the police really can't hold him on speculation."

"But what if they have something to hold him? Then he stuck, right?" Mishon whimpered.

"Me and Rico were there with B last night at your crib, and all I can say is that nigga Mike was still breathing when we left. Trust me."

"It doesn't really matter. I'mma still hold him down. I love Brandon way too much to just let shit ride. I'mma down ass bitch and I'mma do what I gotta do for my man, period."

"I can dig it, and you know if you need anything, just ask," Tomorrow added.

She leaned in and gave Mishon a tight hug. She needed to console her friend, especially since this whole thing was her fault. Deep down, she knew that it was wrong for her to pretend like she had nothing to do with this entire situation, but what could she really say? How could she let her best friend know that not only had she killed Mike, but that she was a stone cold serial killer? Or better yet, how could she let Mishon know that she paid the Highpoint Condominiums' manager Robert to destroy any evidence of her being in the building on the night of Mike's death?

Kane walked into the restaurant and noticed that everyone was surrounding Mishon. He had already heard the news about Brandon, but wondered why no one had called and given him an update.

When he walked over to the table, he slowly exhaled. Kane had some sad news of his own to share.

Tomorrow watched intensely as Kane sat down in the empty chair facing her. She mentally began to prepare herself for what was about to take place. She knew she would have to put on a show.

She tried her best not to acknowledge Kane. Chris ignored him as well. There were still bitter feelings left over from their incident in Ocean City.

"What up, everybody?" Kane interrupted.

Everyone stopped their conversations and stared directly at Kane. He stood before them, looking as if he had a lot on his mind, like perhaps he had something to say. They hoped that what he was about to say was important because they needed to focus on Brandon, but Kane had completely invaded their conversation.

"So umm, I know that a lot has gone on in the last twenty-four hours, but I had to come and let y'all know that Legacy passed away last night." Kane bit his lip in an attempt to keep from crying.

Everyone gasped. With everything that was going on, they couldn't believe that more tragedy had struck within their inner circle.

"Tomorrow, I wanna thank you for helping Legacy get to the ER, but unfortunately, y'all didn't make it in time. She was dead on arrival, they were able to revive her, but her mother decided not to keep her on life support because there was already too much oxygen loss to the brain. The neurologist officially declared her brain dead about three hours ago," Kane explained. "Her mom called me a little while ago and told me she pulled the plug."

Ummm... Crickets! I don't give a fuck about that bitch! Tomorrow thought as she pretended to mourn Legacy's loss.

"You can't be serious! Legacy's dead? What the fuck happened last night?" Mishon quivered.

Tomorrow burst into tears and cried until they created puddles on the table. Chris got up and wrapped his arms around her. When her tears became heavier, he retrieved a napkin from the table's napkin holder and wiped her tears away.

"She called me last night wanting to work things out. We went for a ride and I jumped on the highway. We talked for a minute, but then we got caught up in mad traffic. Y'all know they're building a metro out there. All of a sudden, she started gasping for air and frantically looked for her inhaler. I kept saying *Legacy! Legacy! Are you alright?* She didn't respond, she just kept searching."

Tomorrow paused. She looked up to see if anyone believed her story. Luckily, she was putting on a good show because everyone looked concerned, holding on to her every word. She continued.

"Next thing I know, she lost consciousness and I picked up my phone and dialed 911 and screamed for help. They guided me to the nearest hospital where the medics ran out and took her in. I waited in the lobby for a half an hour while the police asked me a lot of questions. I kept asking the nurse if I could go see her, but they told me that because I wasn't family, they could not disclose any information regarding her situation. I did notify her mom, though. I was gonna wait 'til she got there, but they thought it would be best to call for somebody to come pick me up since I was too shook up to drive. But I didn't know she was dead! I called her mom all night and this morning. I never thought she was going to die. They said she would be fine! I can't believe this, I was such a horrible friend," Tomorrow whined.

Mishon turned and hugged Tomorrow as tight as she could. She understood Tomorrow's pain. Immediately, a sense of guilt filled Mishon's stomach. She and Legacy didn't end on such good terms and now she regretted it. She would never have the chance to squash all of the unnecessary drama, and it made her sick to her stomach.

"I tried to call y'all, nobody would answer the phone. I

didn't know what to do!" Tomorrow continued sobbing.

"Oh my goodness, this is too much to handle. My man is locked up, Mike and Legacy are both dead. My heart can't take it anymore. Kane, please stay in contact. I just want to make sure you're okay. I'mma have to call Legacy's mother to see if she's good. I just can't go to the hospital right now. I'm all over the place."

"No doubt, I'll be in contact with you. Alright y'all I'm out, I got a lot on my mind."

Kane got up from the table and left. He was too devastated to sit and indulge in any more conversation. Even though he fronted like Legacy was nothing more than a ride, no matter what they went through, she secretly held a small place in his heart.

Tomorrow watched as he walked off with his head down. She wiped her face and removed her grieving, remorseful facade.

The waitress walked over and dropped the bill on the table. They all sat quietly not knowing exactly what to say. Chris and Rico threw down a few twenties and motioned for the waitress to pick it up. It was apparent that everyone was overwhelmed and needed to leave, but no one wanted to be the first to walk away.

"So Mishon, you wanna roll with me to get a massage today? After the day we've had, we need it. My treat!" Tomorrow asked.

"Nah, I don't think so. I'mma go rent another room and spend a few more nights there. I just want to be alone and gather my thoughts. You know?"

"Right, I understand. Hey, maybe I can drop by later on tonight to chill? We can smoke and just talk the night away. I will even bring your fave: a deep dish pepperoni pizza." Tomorrow smiled at Mishon.

She tried her best to make Mishon feel better. After all, all of this was Tomorrow's fault. She never meant to get Brandon involved in her mess, but that was just the name of the game, and as for Legacy, well, she had to go.

"Well, that sounds better. Just call me before you come. I'mma get some sleep first."

Everyone got up from the table and exited the restaurant. Rico pulled out a wad of money and handed it to Mishon before parting ways. Chris and Tomorrow followed.

"So what are you about to get into?" Chris asked while walking Tomorrow to her car.

"I think I'mma get some rest too, I had a rough night last night. Plus, class starts soon and I really need a fresh start this time. It's time to focus solely on my school work this semester. You know how my mom is." Tomorrow laughed.

They quickly approached her car. Chris leaned in and gave Tomorrow a long wet kiss. He stared into her eyes.

"Look Mari, you already know I'm feelin' you. I mean damn, a nigga told you he loved you and believe me, I meant it. I been tryna get closer to you ever since we got back from vacation. We been having a great time, but I still feel a little disconnect somewhere, shawty. Let me know what I need to do and I'll do it, where I need to be and I'll be there. I'm willing to do whatever it takes to win your heart."

"You already have, Chris. You know how it goes. It's a work in progress. This is something that's new to both of us, so it's gonna take some time, boo. Just know I'm in it for the long haul."

"I can dig it." Chris kissed Tomorrow again before she unlocked her car door.

She watched Chris walk across the parking lot to his car. She knew that she had to get herself together, and she wanted to do it now more than ever. Tomorrow knew that her love for

Chris would override everything else that she had endured.

Tomorrow made a promise to never kill again. She was going to be on the straight and narrow and start living for Tomorrow. She knew that in order to move forward with Chris, she would have to come clean about everything. She only hoped that her confessions wouldn't backfire.

"I'll tell you what," she called out. "Call me at around four, and maybe we can watch some movies over at your spot," she suggested before getting into her car.

"Sounds good to me, what you wanna see?" he yelled out.

"Umm, how bout Paranormal Activity? Or Precious?" Tomorrow yelled from her car window.

"What the fuck kinda selection is Precious or Paranormal Activity?" Chris joked.

Tomorrow put on her shades and fired her engine.

"Shut up, I hear they're both good and I know your local bootleg man will have them on deck. Stop playing!"

"Aight, bae. I'll see what I can do. Hit me later." Chris frowned.

Tomorrow laughed at Chris' defeated face and pulled out of the parking lot. She briefly looked down and searched for her iPod attachment. She needed to hear some tunes.

After all she had been through; she just wanted to have a nice, quiet and relaxing drive. No one knew what the outcome would be of all the mischief Tomorrow had caused, but if only for this moment, she just wanted to escape the drama.

She turned on her radio and heard Tony Toni Tone's "Just Me and You" blaring through the speakers. She giggled to herself before adjusting her rearview mirror.

"You thought it was over, bitch?"

CHAPTER

~ 21 ~

O h bitch, don't look so fucking surprised."

Tomorrow stared intensely into Quan's eyes from her rearview mirror. She couldn't believe that she had been caught slipping again. She thought that she at least had a few more weeks before he showed his face, but she was so wrong.

Quan had rage and revenge in his eyes. He had waited months to finally get his hands on Tomorrow. She had ruined his life and made him look like a fool, not to mention that she had cut him so deeply that there were physical markings left on his face as a reminder of his embarrassment.

Because these marks would last forever, Quan awoke daily with hatred in his heart for Tomorrow. She would have to pay for what she had done to him. She would have to die.

Tomorrow started to turn around and face Quan, but she froze when she heard a familiar clicking sound.

"Keep your eyes on the fucking road, bitch. Now you're gonna keep driving until I tell you to stop, and don't try nothin' funny, or I'll splatter your fucking brains out. Do you understand?" Quan yelled.

Tomorrow remained silent.

"Oh, now you ain't got all that fuckin' mouth that you had before, huh bitch? You scared, huh? You was a bad muthafucka with that blade, but you ain't got shit to say now, bitch!"

"Where you want me to go?" Tomorrow sighed.

"Turn right here." Quan got close to the back of her head and held the gun there. He sniffed her locs and was enamored by the mango smell.

"Mmm, you still smell good. I'mma enjoy fucking you once I kill you, bitch."

Tomorrow quivered. She couldn't stand the fact that Quan was so close to her, sniffing her like a pervert. The fact that he had the upper hand only angered her more, but she did what he said.

After about twenty minutes of driving, Quan instructed Tomorrow to pull into a vacant parking lot. Tomorrow had no clue where she was, but she knew she was somewhere in Maryland. Behind the parking lot was a building that looked as if it were condemned.

"Now get out of the car and don't make no sudden moves, bitch," Quan directed as he exited the back seat of the car and pointed the gun at Tomorrow.

Tomorrow did as she was told. She exited the car and faced the building. Quan placed the gun at her temple and told her to walk through the door.

The building was dark, but Quan seemingly knew his way around. He pushed Tomorrow into one of the building's empty rooms. A little light shined through a space between two of the wooden boards that were nailed to the windows.

"Sit yo' fancy ass down, bitch!" Quan yelled.

He hit Tomorrow over the head with the butt of his gun and watched as she dropped to the floor. He quickly pulled out a pair of handcuffs from his pocket and cuffed Tomorrow to the old rusty desk that sat across the room.

When she awoke, Tomorrow saw Quan standing before her laughing. She was naked and handcuffed to the old desk. Her body ached and she could barely move.

A salty taste slipped across her tongue, and that's when she realized what Quan had done.

"How my cum taste, bitch? I just nutted all down your fucking throat. I shoulda nutted in yo' eye so you could watch my kids, bitch!" Quan laughed at his own joke.

He slapped Tomorrow in the face with his dick and laughed again. He was getting a kick out of having his way with her, knowing that there was nothing she could do about it.

Tomorrow tried to spit out every drop but she couldn't escape the taste.

"I'm going to fucking kill you, you bitch ass nigga!" Tomorrow screamed.

Quan punched her in the face and watched the blood fly from her mouth.

"You're gonna regret the day you ever crossed my path," Tomorrow continued. "You can bet that."

Quan put the gun to Tomorrow's temple and held it in place. He wanted to see the fear in her eyes. The same fear that he had when he begged for his life. But she refused to show any emotion.

"I should just kill you right now, bitch. You fucked with

the wrong nigga this time. I just wanted to fuck your uppity ass, but you just had to take this shit to a whole new level. I can't let you get away with that shit!" Quan screamed.

"Beg for your muthafuckin' life, bitch!" he continued.

Tomorrow refused. He kicked her in the stomach as hard as he could. She moaned in pain, but refused to beg for her life. She figured that if she was going to die, she was going to die with some dignity. She wouldn't die letting Quan know he had the upper hand.

"Nigga, fuck you. If you gonna kill me, then kill me, you pussy ass nigga. You can't even kill a muthafucka the right way. Matter of fact, you should just uncuff me. I have a rope in my car and you can just hang yourself with it. You're a worthless piece of shit, no one would give a damn anyway!" Tomorrow taunted him.

Quan slapped Tomorrow across the face. In a rage, he kept slapping her until he ran out of breath. Once he was done, he looked down at her and noticed she had an evil smirk on her face.

"Bitch, what the fuck is so funny?" Quan yelled.

Tomorrow could feel the blood trickling from her face. She knew that Quan would eventually kill her, but she wasn't going to go out like a punk. She would be Tomorrow until her last breath.

"Nigga, you're pathetic. I've spent my whole life around stupid niggas like you tryna prove they hard, but really they ain't shit and ain't never gonna be shit. I've killed niggas like you without a second thought, and yet, you in here on some fucking lifetime movie network shit."

"Bitch, you ain't never killed nobody. Shut that shit up!" Quan laughed.

"You must not watch the news, nigga."

"Oh so now you that serial killer bitch, huh?"

236

"Check my pockets." Tomorrow giggled.

Quan was skeptical about reaching into Tomorrow's pockets. After what she had pulled the last time, he didn't know what she was capable of.

"Don't be scared." Tomorrow laughed harder.

Quan reached into her pocket and pulled out her Tom Ford Scarlet Rouge lipstick.

"This shit, bitch? What does that prove?"

"I forgot yo' ass was a fucking dummy!"

"Shut up, bitch, what's the point?"

"I've killed 15 men so far. I fucked them, killed them, and placed kisses on their foreheads. I'm telling you this because once I kill you, you'll get the same treatment. So take my advice, you need to man the fuck up, nigga! Cuz trust me, if you don't kill me, I'm going to kill you. No question." Tomorrow laughed.

"That's it, bitch!" Quan yelled as he pointed the gun at Tomorrow's

His hand shivered uncontrollably. He had never killed anyone before, but the adrenaline rushing through him let him know that he was indeed ready. Tomorrow had taken this to a new level, and now he would have to prove that he was more than just talk.

Quan cocked the gun and prepared to shoot. He looked down at Tomorrow with a victorious grin.

"Any last words?" He smiled.

"Fuck yourself." Tomorrow laughed.

BOOM!

A single shot was fired, and Quan immediately dropped to the floor. It took Tomorrow a minute to realize what had just happened. There was now a pool of blood forming from his lifeless body.

Tomorrow saw the fresh bullet hole in Quan's head and wondered what had just happened. Was she dead? Was she hallucinating?

She looked up and saw Chris holding a smoking gun in his left hand. He waited a second to make sure that Quan was dead before dropping his gun to the ground. Chris ran over to Tomorrow and un-cuffed her.

"Baby, how did you—" Tomorrow started to say.

"I told you. I always got you, boo. Forever, " he replied.

Before they exited, Chris grabbed the lipstick off the ground and drew an X across Quan's forehead.

"Damn, my baby is a fuckin' killer." He laughed to himself.

"No, ex killer," Tomorrow corrected him.

"Yeah, aight. We'll see."

EPILOGUE
THREE YEARS LATER

Tomorrow walked into her two-bedroom luxury condo and plopped onto her leather couch. She had been working all day and was happy to finally be home. She slid off her black Gucci pumps and turned on the television.

"Baby, you here?" Chris yelled out from the master bedroom.

"Yea."

Chris came out of the room and walked down to the hall. He went over to the couch and placed a kiss on Tomorrow's lips. He sat down next to her and grabbed her feet.

"Mmm, baby, a foot massage. You're so good to me."

Things had been good for Tomorrow and Chris. Tomorrow was finishing up her senior year in college and had landed an internship at the Washington Psychological Center in Northwest D.C. Soon, they would be offering her a full-time position there, which would allow her to get all of the information she needed to finally publish her book.

Chris was the head of operations at a major construction site in D.C., and they were living a picture-perfect life. Almost perfect.

"Here, baby, you got this letter in the mail today. Open it up." Chris smiled. He held out his hand.

"Look at you, all nosey and shit," Tomorrow joked.

She snatched the letter from Chris' hand and opened it. Her smile quickly turned from a smile into a frown when she read the words pasted across the paper.

PEOPLE DIE, SECRETS DON'T!!!

Tomorrow handed Chris the paper. He mouthed the words and looked at her with a stern but shocked stare. She couldn't believe this was happening. It had been three years since she killed anyone and she thought that she had done a good job of covering up all of her tracks.

Tomorrow had purged all of her sins, at least the ones that she thought she needed to cast away. Because of her love for Chris, she made a vow that she would no longer kill, and she had actually stuck to it. Between church, therapy, and her bi-weekly support group meetings, Tomorrow had done everything she could to fight her self-induced urges. And now this?

Why couldn't they just leave well enough alone? Tomorrow hadn't hurt anyone in a very long time and wanted to leave the past in the past. Covering up evidence had proved to be difficult enough, but now someone knew her secret and was threatening to reveal it. How could she ever stop them when a) she didn't know who they were, and b) she had made a vow not to kill?

"Baby, don't let this shit get to you. Whoever it is, we will find them and we will handle it," Chris assured her.

"How? We have no clue who the fuck sent it." Tomorrow looked down and noticed that the person had added a nonsense return address.

Guess Who
5101 Secrets Lane
Lipstick, Va 22301

"I said, we'll handle it."

The sounds of shattering glass and alarms snapped Tomorrow and Chris out of their conversation. Tomorrow knew that the sound she heard was her own car alarm.

Both she and Chris ran out as fast as they could and made their way to her BMW. They both stood with their mouths wide open when they got a view of what happened.

Pictures of all of the "Kiss of Death" murders lay plastered all over Tomorrow's car. Someone had been following Tomorrow for years and had seen all of the bad things she had done. Now they wanted everyone else to see them as well.

Tomorrow felt the blood boil within her. She had to know who was causing all of this madness and she needed to know now. She got even more upset when she noticed that the pictures were intentionally placed and glued to the roof of her car so that she couldn't quickly remove them.

240

Who had done this? Slowly but surely, she was losing a grip on reality and on the promise she made to not only Chris, but to herself and God.

Chris noticed the brick that lay on Tomorrow's passenger seat. He opened her door and grabbed it. There was another letter wrapped around the brick.

...P.S. Game on Bitch!

www.ingramcontent.com/pod-product-compliance
Lightning Source LLC
Chambersburg PA
CBHW070054260626
47160CB00004B/1203